The Celebration Family

The Celebration Family

Diane Nason
with
Birdie Etchison

THOMAS NELSON PUBLISHERS
Nashville • Camden • New York

Second printing

Published in Nashville, Tennessee, by Thomas Nelson, Inc. and distributed in
Canada by Lawson Falle, Ltd., Cambridge, Ontario.

Printed in the United States of America.

Scripture quotes are from THE NEW KING JAMES VERSION. Copyright © 1979,
1980, 1982, Thomas Nelson, Inc., Publishers

Library of Congress Cataloging in Publication Data

Nason, Diane.
  The celebration family.

  1. Nason, Dennis. 2. Nason, Diane. 3. Foster
parents—Oregon—Biography. 4. Family—Oregon—
Religious aspects—Christianity—Case studies.
5. Adoption—Oregon—Case studies. I. Etchison,
Birdie L., 1937-   . II. Title.
HQ759.7.N37 1983   306.8'7   83-17440
ISBN 0-8407-5849-9

To my father and mother, who
have loved their grandchildren
so deeply.

To Dr. Bill Miller, for his
never-ending encouragement,
advice, and love.

And to the most beautiful
little angel in Heaven—
Nicole—Grandma will always
love you.

Contents

Foreword

When first contacted by the Nason family to assist in their efforts to bring home little Danny from El Salvador, I had the deep sense that this was no ordinary family and that their request was not going to be routine. The more exposure I had to the Nasons, the more I knew my assessment was correct. This family has a uniqueness that sets it apart from any other I have known.

The Celebration Family is a travelogue of a journey with the ultimate destination being the unity of human beings of all races, nationalities and levels of ability. It is a pilgrimage fueled by faith in the Lord and the belief in the sanctity of every life. It is an expedition that extends far beyond the pages of this book into the hearts of all who hear about the Nasons' commitment and their unique children.

This is also a story of a family who knows defeat but who is never defeated; who knows each individual needs to function within the boundaries of a family whose life is boundless.

Many of the children who have "come home" to the Nasons arrived with severe obstacles to overcome, includ-

ing cultural and language barriers and physical and psychological handicaps—problems which for some may
never be corrected. The true healing made possible by the
Nasons is the mending of broken hearts and the restoration
of broken spirits through love and faith, without which no
challenge or disability can be successfully overcome.

Of great interest is the way in which this story maps the
progression of the expanding human heart. Beginning with
the great odds against them in marrying at an early age, in
the illness of their first child, and then in the adoptions,
often against the wishes of family and local officials, the
Nasons were able, in each case, to convince all doubters
that they would never flag in the certainty of their mission.
They were confident they had been chosen to press ahead.
Lacking room, lacking money, they nevertheless knew this
journey must continue.

The Celebration Family should be required reading for all
who are considering adoption, particularly of hard-to-
place children. It will convince the reader that children are
hard to place only in one's mind, not in one's heart. Would
that we had a nation of Nasons.

MARK O. HATFIELD
U.S. Senator (R.–Oregon)

Mark	home-grown
Scott	home-grown
Lisa	home-grown
Lori	Oregon
Katie	Oregon
Bill	Oregon
Kari	Vietnam
Kecia	Vietnam
*Marie	New York
Theresa	New York
Sheila and Sherry	Texas
Donny	home-grown
Danny	El Salvador
Melissa	Indiana
Gary	Washington
Kim	Washington
David	New York
Mandy	India
Diana	home-grown
Daryl	El Salvador
*Marty	New York
Jeff	New York
Kenny	home-grown
Dorell and Darin	New York
Kevin	Florida
Cindy	Georgia
Billy Joe	Indiana
Nancie	India
Bobby	New York
Richie	Brazil

Meet the Nasons

*deceased

Meet the Nasons

I had heard about the Nasons of Sisters, Oregon. They were a family with six biological children and had adopted a total of twenty-six more.

I was coming to live in their home for a few days, and my feelings were mixed. Who would want to adopt such a gang of kids? One child, maybe. Two, possibly. But twenty-six! And then I realized the burning question was not *who* would do it, but *how* did they do it? And *why*?

It was mid-April, and the city I had left was blossoming and bursting with spring. But the small community of Sisters, with its snowcapped peaks dominating the background, hadn't yet awakened from winter. Cool, crisp air filled my lungs as I drove slowly down the lane from the road to the house, passing the barn and pasture where several cows grazed. I paused under a huge sign extending overhead:

PLAINVIEW DAIRY
THE NASONS

A few hundred yards in the distance, a two-story ranch house sprawled against the sky. I had arrived.

I had halfway expected a scene of bedlam and noise, perhaps with kids pouring out the windows, but the house was quiet. I timidly knocked.

A small boy, about eight, dropped a water hose and raced across the yard to greet me. I'd studied photos of the children before I left home, and my mind frantically searched for the right name to put with this dark face with flashing brown eyes. He must be one of the boys from El Salvador, but which one?

"Hi, are you Danny or Daryl?" I asked.

He grinned shyly. "I'm Danny. Mom's inside—" At that moment, the front door swung open and the woman I'd come to meet stood there, smiling.

"Hello, I'm Diane Nason. We've been expecting you. Come on in."

Diane, her long, black hair pulled back with barrettes, could, at first glance, pass as one of the kids. I liked her immediately.

Within minutes, I met four grade-schoolers, five preschoolers and kindergarteners, and four babies in diapers.

Kecia, a darling eight-year-old Vietnamese with bouncy pony tails, suddenly asked where the pool table had gone.

"To the church, don't you remember?" Diane responded.

Kecia looked dismayed. "And what about the Ping-Pong table?"

"Same place," her mother answered.

"But, I *liked* that pool table," she said.

"There was no room for it, Kecia. The two cribs had to go in the family room. Besides, what would you rather have, a pool table or a new brother and sister?" Diane asked.

Without changing her expression, Kecia answered, "A pool table."

Diane laughed—something she does frequently. Her laugh is hearty, contagious. "It figures," she said, with a shrug of her shoulders.

Later, she zipped into the kitchen and whipped up a three-gallon bowl of pudding and prepared a platter full of sliced bread with butter while I wrote the date and mileage in my notebook.

At 5:15 in the evening, the door opened and Dennis was home.

"Daddy's home! Daddy's home!" several voices cried as he was surrounded by a sea of arms and legs.

I extended a hand to a short, burly man with friendly eyes, and wondered about this remarkable person—the man whom thirty children lovingly call "Daddy."

"Daddy, come wrestle with us," Donny begged.

"Later, son."

"Hey, Dad, can we meet for lunch one day next week?" twelve-year-old Katie Sue asked. "I just want to talk to you. . . ."

Dennis pulled out a chair and sat down. "I'm sure that can be arranged."

"I brought a library book home," David said, holding up a book.

"We'll read it as soon as dinner is over."

When two-year-old Kenny turned away from his bowl of meaty beef stew at the dinner table, Dennis scooped him onto his lap and coaxed him into trying a few bites.

I began to see what a smooth team Diane and Dennis make. Diane appears to be in charge. She issues orders, outlines the daily job details, charts the course, while Dennis quietly, lovingly makes certain the navigation goes smoothly.

In the course of my visit, I discovered much more about *how* this huge family manages. Theirs is a story of meeting needs on a daily basis, of fighting bureaucratic red tape to enable a child to join their home (even if it means contacting a United States senator for help), of having expenses miraculously met, of being disappointed and heartbroken, and of loving children and teaching them to love in return.

Above all, I discovered something about *why* this family exists—why they can live each day as a celebration family.

As in all stories, there are beginnings . . .

Birdie Etchison

Chapter One

Love Story

The summer of 1951 brought new adventure and excitement to a family of six living in a bustling suburb of southern California.

The family consisted of Don Fehlman, wife Lyn, three boys, Bob and Richard, nearly grown, Jerry, sixteen, and dark-eyed Diane Louise.

At age eight, Diane was the apple of her daddy's eye, and he wanted her to share in his lifelong dream of living on a ranch. The dream ended up being 2,500 acres in northern California, a few miles from the Oregon border.

Apprehensive about the move, Lyn protested mildly. "But, what about Diane's violin lessons?"

"She'll love the ranch and won't even miss the violin," he said.

He was correct.

Enthralled with the huge spread, Diane exchanged violins for horses, sidewalks for riding trails.

The house, a renovated hotel, boasted nine bedrooms.

Enchanted, Diane raced from room to room. "Which bedroom is mine?" she asked.

"Take your pick," her mother replied.

Finally, Diane chose a large, airy room with four big windows overlooking the horse pasture. A box elder branch reached the window and Diane soon discovered that climbing out onto the large limb and sliding down the tree to the ground below was fun. The fact that hundreds of tiny bugs covered her didn't stop her for a moment.

The monstrous, second-story bathroom with two windows also provided an escape route via a small porch and another stout, sturdy limb of a tree.

The dry land with rolling hills dotted with juniper, scrub oak and sage brush offered many exploring possibilities for Diane. Huge rock formations were part of the territory, and one day while investigating the many nooks and crannies, Diane discovered the rattlesnake den.

Going to school was a new adventure. The first two years in her new home, Diane attended a one-room country schoolhouse. The following year, she caught the school bus at the end of the driveway and rode fifteen miles into town each day for school.

The Fehlmans soon discovered they couldn't make the ranch a working proposition, so Diane's father went back to teaching math and science in the Yreka High School. Still it was a struggle to make the mortgage payment, and Don talked about selling the ranch.

"Dad, you won't sell the ranch, will you?" Jerry asked. "You know I'm going in the Air Force, and I want something to come home to."

"No, we won't sell," Don promised.

Lyn went back to teaching, too. While Don's earnings covered everyday expenses, her salary made the mortgage payment on the ranch.

Diane was alone a lot now. She felt like an only child with Jerry gone.

She knew it was hard for her mother to keep the house

and to teach, so Diane tried to help. Mornings she rose early and coaxed a fire to start in the big, old woodstove.

Often she cleaned the whole hotel from top to bottom. It was fun and she liked to keep busy. She also moved to a different bedroom every month.

Free times were spent riding horseback on the ranch, uphill and down. Diane graduated from Citation, a mild-mannered pony, to Domi, a frisky little jumper she had trained from a foal.

Diane sensed God's presence at an early age and talked openly and freely with Him. She attended the Baptist church with her parents and couldn't remember a time when the Lord hadn't been part of her life. But there was something commanding about the beauty of nature, the freedom of being alone that added a depth to her Christian life. She felt a deeper sense of belonging, a real closeness to the Lord in the mountainous ranch setting.

"What do you do when you're gone so long?" her mother asked one cloudless summer day.

"I just ride and ride. Sometimes I sing at the top of my lungs and I think God likes that."

"I'm sure He does," her mother answered.

It was that freedom in praising God that was to be a building point for Diane's future, though she didn't know it then. One time God told Diane she would have four sons and two daughters, but she didn't tell her mother about that. It was something she wanted to keep to herself. It seemed special.

The years on the ranch were formative ones. Diane led an active life. She was a doer, independent. She could do anything she set her mind to. Like sewing. Her mother handed her a dress pattern, and she figured it out by herself.

Diane's love for and interest in horses intensified. She participated in horse shows from the time she was ten. She won in all the events she entered: pole bending, racing, barrel racing, jumping. In her sophomore year of high school, Diane was captain of the Lancerets, an all-girl drill team, and traveled all over California and Oregon.

"I don't know how you manage to be so active in the Lancerets and still keep up your schoolwork," her mother said.

Diane smiled. She kept busy, rarely studied, and still brought home straight A's. "All I know is, I want to ride in rodeos forever," she declared.

By now, the large ranch had become nothing but a burden to the Fehlmans. They decided to retire, and chose Ashland, Oregon. Situated in the foothills of the Siskiyou Mountains, Ashland was only forty-five minutes away, and best of all, Southern Oregon College was there. There would certainly be more cultural advantages for Diane.

In September 1959 Don and Lyn purchased a house in Ashland. Since they had to sell the ranch first, they rented the new house to a couple with the stipulation that Diane could live there with them and start her junior year at high school in Ashland.

Diane looked forward to the move. It was a new and exciting adventure as she had never lived in town before. Later, however, Diane would discover how much she missed the ranch, the quiet peacefulness and the closeness with God and nature.

"Diane, we need to throw a party so you can meet some of the kids," her cousin Linda suggested one Saturday shortly after Diane had moved to Ashland.

The party sounded like a good idea. The two girls had pored over the school yearbook, and every time Diane asked about a certain guy, Linda would comment, "He's not your type," or, "He's going steady," or, "He doesn't like girls."

Then came a picture of a cute guy with dark, curly hair and dark eyes. "What about this one?" Diane asked.

"Oh, that's Dennis. Dennis Nason. Yeah, he's nice—popular too. And into sports," Linda added, "football and wrestling."

"Let's ask him," Diane suggested.

"Okay. Good idea."

But they didn't see Dennis the next few days of school. The party was scheduled for the coming Saturday. Then, one afternoon when both girls were in the library, Linda suddenly nudged Diane. "That's him," she said, pointing.

Diane recognized him immediately. He looked just like his picture.

"Go on, give him the invitation," Linda urged.

"No, *you* do it," Diane said, giving her cousin a shove.

Diane was not usually shy, but it was a new school and things were different here.

Linda walked over and invited Dennis to the party.

He glanced at Diane and smiled. "Yeah, sure. I'd love to come."

Diane knew from that moment that Dennis was *the one*, and that party was the first step in their relationship.

Dennis had the same feelings about Diane too. Walking out of the library with his best friend, he remarked, "I'm going to marry that girl someday."

The *someday* came sooner than they realized.

They were totally compatible, totally enthralled with each other, and soon fell in love. Dennis and Diane became engaged in February 1960, their junior year of high school.

The Fehlmans tried to talk them out of getting married. "You're too young to be serious," her mother said. "Besides, there's college to think about—not marriage and babies."

"It's a big step," her father added. "One you want to be sure about."

"I am," Diane said emphatically. "I've got it all figured out. I'll have enough credits to graduate at the end of my junior year. Dennis can go back to school to finish while I go to work."

While the Fehlmans didn't like the idea, Dennis's mom and stepdad were vehemently opposed since Dennis was underage.

There were various comments from teachers and class-mates.

"You're both too young," was the most frequent remark.

"Why get married now? Why not wait for a year or so?"

"Do you *have* to get married?"

Sure they were young, and there were a lot of years ahead of them, but no, it was not a "have to" case. They loved each other and didn't want to wait. Dennis was only seventeen, but he had matured at a young age. With a chronically ill mother, he bore the responsibilities of taking care of a younger sister and helping out around the house.

When the Fehlmans saw that Diane's mind was made up, they relented. They knew she was responsible and mature. However, Diane and her mother wanted a church wedding with white gown and all the finery. Dennis's mother reluc-tantly agreed and presented the young couple with her set of wedding and engagement rings.

Neither Dennis nor Diane realized that Oregon had a law stating that marriage could not be performed when both parties were under eighteen (unless the girl was pregnant). With their mothers, Dennis and Diane drove over the state line—back to the town near the ranch where Diane had spent so many happy years—and were married by a Cal-ifornia justice of the peace on June 15. Then they drove back to Ashland to wait for the ceremony on June 26, 1960. Staying apart for those days was difficult, but they did it.

God had a plan for their lives, though they didn't realize it then. God needed not one, but two willing servants—two people totally and completely committed to each other and sharing their joys and sorrows.

Their first apartment, a one-room duplex with outdoor plumbing, bunk beds, and a small hotplate for cooking, was more than adequate for Dennis and Diane. All they knew was that whatever they did, no matter where they lived or how much money they had, they wanted to do it together.

"We have each other," Diane said. "We'll learn, grow and love, and most important, experience God's provision."

They didn't own a car, so Dennis walked to school. Diane walked to her daytime job at the A&W, and each evening they strolled together to their job at the local theater. Diane was cashier while Dennis ushered.

No, there wasn't a lot of planning, but there was faith and a knowledge that God was in charge and things would work out.

But things were not automatically smooth for the newlyweds. Their first fight occurred just a few months after they were married. They had one hundred dollars in the bank, and Dennis wanted to take Diane out to dinner. In 1960 a good meal for two could be had for ten dollars. Dennis went to the bank and started to withdraw the ten dollars, only to learn that Diane had been in earlier and taken out seventy-five dollars.

Dennis stormed out of the bank and headed for home. His Irish temper was showing as he entered the small apartment sounding like a raging bull.

"And just where is the seventy-five dollars you took out of the account without asking me?"

Diane stared in disbelief. She had never seen this side of

Dennis—the angry side. "I . . . I didn't know it would make you mad," she finally answered. "I only wanted to surprise you."

He shook his head. "You surprised me all right. What did you do with the money?"

"I needed seventy-five dollars for an entry fee in the rodeo."

"Seventy-five dollars!" Dennis exploded. "That's a ton of money!"

"I know," Diane said calmly, "but so is three hundred dollars if I win."

Diane not only won the three-hundred-dollar prize, but she also brought home a silver buckle, a saddle, and a huge trophy. Her feat? All-around point winner in all events, including barrel racing, jumps, goat-tying and pole-bending.

From time to time the young couple talked about having a family. They even discussed the possibility of adopting children. They were open to God's leading. They didn't realize that not only would they bring new life into the world, but that they would also have a large part in sustaining the lives of children already born.

Eighteen months after their marriage, Dennis and Diane looked forward to their firstborn. The Lord's master plan was beginning. That first child and the agonizing years of handling his severe illness were the foundation of things to come.

And as the Lord led them down the rocky path He had designed and chosen for them, He knew they would succeed because of their love and commitment to each other and their growing faith and trust in Him.

Chapter Two

The First Three "Home-Growns"

I'm sorry, Mrs. Nason, but you're going to have to remove carpeting, curtains and all toys from Mark's bedroom. . . .

Diane stared at the letter, tears rising in her eyes, not believing what she had just read.

Your son, Mark Nason, has three types of skin problems: scaly skin, an inherited congenital type of skin surface; cradle-cap eczema; and allergic-type eczema. Of the inhalant tests conducted, Mark reacted to horse dander, house-dust. . . .

Diane raced to the phone and called Dennis at work. "It came. The letter came," she finally said.

"What did it say?"

"That Mark has allergies."

"We already know that," Dennis said. "You mean we made that long trip to Portland and lived through three days of tests just to hear—"

"No," Diane broke in. "There's more to it."

"What, then?"

Diane felt tears welling up again. What was wrong with her? So much had happened recently. Mark had been ill since his birth in November 1961—first the rash that eventually covered his entire body, then the severe asthma attacks. She was now six months pregnant and elated that she had carried the baby this long. There had been a miscarriage a year ago, and she had cried over the lost child. Dennis had tried to reassure her that there would be more children, but she hadn't been so sure.

"Diane, are you okay?" Dennis was asking.

"Yes, it's just that he has to have tar baths every day and shots three times a week to desensitize him." Diane hesitated. "Besides that, we have to get rid of everything in Mark's bedroom, and the specialist said to give the animals away. Mark cannot tolerate any type of horse or dog dander, dust, or *anything*."

Dennis whistled. "That's rough. No wonder you're down. Wish I could come home, but you know how jobs are."

Yes, Diane knew how it was. It was a struggle trying to keep up with rising medical bills. If only Mark weren't so sick. The asthma wasn't improving, but she felt there must be a doctor *somewhere* with the answers.

Diane picked up the receiver again. "Daddy? Would you come over and take down Mark's bed?"

"What on earth for?" Don Fehlman asked.

"I have to take everything out of his room. That's what the specialist said."

"Sure, honey. Be right there."

Mark called out from the bedroom, where he'd been napping. "Mommy, I not feel good."

Diane sat on the edge of his bed and wiped his forehead. Already his breathing was raspy. "I know, honey, but just hang in there. We're going to make it so you'll get better. You'll see."

His big brown eyes grew wide. "No shots?"

Diane sighed. "Oh, Mark, I don't know. It all depends on what Dr. Bill says."

Dr. Bill Miller had taken care of Mark since his first asthma attack at eighteen months of age. He met Diane at the hospital and administered adrenalin shots to Mark, pulling him through a major attack a year later. It was Dr. Bill who suggested the specialist, in hopes that Mark could be helped.

Don Fehlman came in with a screwdriver. "I'll have the bed down in a jif."

"My bed!" Mark cried. "That my bed!"

A tightness went through Diane. "I know, sweetie, but you have to sleep on a little mattress. Daddy will buy you a new bed."

"The horse has to go," Diane said, not looking at her parents. She couldn't remember a time without a horse.

"And the other animals?"

"We can keep the dog and cats outside."

"The horse is already outside," her father said.

"But if we can't ride, what's the point of keeping him?" Diane's voice trailed off. One of her biggest dreams was to dress Mark up in a cowboy outfit and teach him to ride. He could have ridden in the Junior Rodeo someday. But that dream would never come true—no horse, no rodeo, no cute bedroom.

"You might try changing your clothes before coming back to the house," her father suggested.

"Oh, Daddy, maybe that *is* a solution." Diane's hand rested on her abdomen. *Maybe this new little life could ride the horse. Surely the Lord wouldn't send her another critically ill child. How could she manage? There were only so many hours in the day, and Mark took so much of her time. What if this baby were sick?* No, she wouldn't think about it. She had never dwelled on negative thoughts and she wasn't going to start now. She'd thought she couldn't take care of Mark those first few months, but the Lord knew she could, and she had.

Dennis worked until two each morning, and he always found Diane sitting up, holding Mark's hands so he wouldn't scratch himself. Dennis would offer to hold Mark so Diane could get some sleep.

"But you need your sleep too," she'd say, lifting her face for his kiss. "I can manage."

"You know how I need to unwind," he'd answer, taking Mark into his arms.

Dennis was still going to school and working at the theater part-time. More recently he had started cooking at the local country club. As he was also going to start work at the post office, he decided to drop the theater job.

Dennis would sit for an hour, holding Mark, and sometimes a tear slid down his cheek. This child, so much a part of him and Diane, had suffered so much. They'd expected a healthy, normal, beautiful baby, but Mark simply wasn't healthy. Yet with his big, dark eyes, black hair and pale skin, he was beautiful to them.

Sometimes Dennis questioned God. "Why us? Why Mark? Is there some blue sky ahead?" He didn't feel close to the Lord anymore. It was impossible to attend church with his Sunday working hours, and Diane couldn't take Mark to any of the services. He was too sick and fussy. They couldn't have company over, as the least bit of activity triggered an asthma attack for Mark.

Dr. Bill shook his head the first time he saw Mark. "In all my years of practice, I've never seen such an aggravated case of eczema. How long has he been like this?"

"Since he was five days old," Diane said.

Now as Diane looked at her small son, lying on the sim-

ple mattress with white sheet and blanket as prescribed by
the specialist, she couldn't believe any of this. He was ill,
but his spirit was beautiful. Often she would find herself
crying, and Mark would reach out his little hand and touch
her arm. "It's okay, Mommy. I not hurt too much."

She knew that the Lord had sent this special little boy for
a reason. The reason wasn't clear just yet, but there would
be an explanation someday. In the meantime, she would
carry on and pray that somewhere, someone would have an
answer to Mark's condition.

Dennis Scott Nason was born March 21, 1964, and the
minute Diane looked into the tiny, puckered-up face, her
heart swelled with gladness.

"Dennis, did you see those *shoulders*? He looks just like
you," she cried. "A little Nason."

But the thing Diane most noticed was the clear, pink
skin, the healthy color, the lusty crying. God had heard and
answered her prayers. Her fears of having a second unhealthy child were unfounded.

At two months, Scott's black hair fell out and was replaced by a reddish-blond fuzz that stuck straight up.

"Looks like a little chicken," Dennis said, reaching down
and ruffling his son's hair.

Diane laughed, because Scott did look funny, but he was
so healthy she could never stop being thankful.

"This child is amazing," Diane said to Dr. Bill. "Can you
imagine, no allergies?"

He nodded. "That's why we're going to put him on solids
now. I'm sure he'll do just great."

Other than a mild reaction to orange juice, Scott did
great.

Mark was jealous of Scott, but Diane had expected that.
Wasn't it normal? Mark was used to being the center of her

universe, with Dennis gone most of the time. Then along comes a totally new stranger and Mommy was doing lots of things for him, spending time with him when Mark needed her.

One day Mark asked why Scott was different.

"Different?" Diane asked.

"Well, Scott doesn't have all these itchies all over him," was Mark's reply.

Diane looked away as she scooped Mark into her lap. "Well, Mark, God just made Scotty different, but He made you *very special*."

"I know," he said, in the adult way of talking, "but I wish I didn't have all of this . . ."

O, Lord, Diane thought. *Why does Mark suffer? If only I could understand.*

While Scott wasn't sick with asthma or allergies, he did have another problem: he was accident prone.

"I can't believe all these accidents," Diane exclaimed to Dennis. "He goes around with a black eye and bruises—looks like he's been in a prize fight!"

"He's just so active and curious about everything," Dennis said.

"Plus a little clumsy!" Diane added.

Scott wasn't rushed to the emergency room with asthma attacks. He arrived with sprained ankles, gashes on his forehead, and cuts on his upper lip.

Diane had another miscarriage at four months when Scott was a year old, and had to stay in the hospital for a few days. "I wish I could say it doesn't matter," she told Dennis, "but it does. Very much."

"I understand," Dennis said, holding her close.

Mark's trips to the hospital continued, but Diane discovered she could treat the milder attacks at home with a Bird machine—a medicated inhalant machine hooked up to an oxygen tank, with a face mask covering the nose and mouth, forcing the patient to breathe. She also learned to give Mark shots and to force up the phlegm that collected in his chest by pounding on his back with a certain motion of the sides of her hand.

Still, there were two or three trips a week to the hospital. Diane learned about hospital life during those visits, knowledge that would prove invaluable later.

"It's like a city complete within itself," Diane remarked to Dennis one day. "There's joy, sadness, birth and death. People become dependent upon each other, and those in the medical profession have great compassion."

The nurses tried to make Mark's life as close to life outside as possible. They treated him like a visitor in their home, like a friend.

Diane learned medical terminology during those hours. She came into contact with many different illnesses. She saw children enter the hospital and she noticed that some didn't leave.

Since Mark could be thrown into a violent attack from the physical activity of play, he had to stay quiet, and the Nasons didn't dare risk having children come over. They didn't visit friends either, as people usually owned dogs and cats, and Mark would immediately start wheezing. Some of the friends didn't understand, and there were often hurt feelings.

It was a lesson for the Nasons on withdrawing into their own close family unit—being interdependent. They drew closer as a result of Mark's illness, instead of growing apart as often happens when illness hits a family.

As always, Diane's parents helped out. Grandpa Fehlman taught Mark to play checkers, chess and old maid. Sometimes he'd tell a story, using a puppet he'd made from driftwood. Mark especially liked the tales that continued from one episode to another. He also took Mark fishing—something Mark could do, since there were no fur, feathers, or dander to provoke his asthma.

Scott loved animals, and at last Diane had a little boy to dress up in cowboy boots and set up on a horse. He couldn't have pets in the house, but outdoors he had rabbits, a few chickens, a couple of stray cats, and (his favorite) a dog.

It was a busy, hectic time for Dennis. He wanted to spend more time with his family, but it wasn't possible. There were so many bills to be paid—an awesome responsibility for a young man. He had begun working at the post office, learning everything on his own. The mounting expenses eventually forced him to drop out of college after three years, and he made another decision that affected all their lives. He gave up his dream to teach school and became a full-time postal employee.

"One of these days I'll give up the cooking job too," Dennis said.

"I'm all for that," Diane answered, slipping her arm around Dennis. "Did I ever tell you that I love you?"

"A hundred times, but tell me again."

Six months after the miscarriage, Diane again became pregnant.

"Maybe we'll get a girl," she said. "But most important, I'm praying for a healthy baby, one I can carry full term."

"Perhaps you should consider this to be your last child," the doctor suggested. "With the tendency toward asthma, your miscarriages and difficult births, it's something to think about."

"We've always planned to adopt anyway," Diane told her doctor.

The pregnancy was difficult, more so as Diane was wakened nearly every night by a fretful Mark.

"Mommy," he'd cry out.

Diane was tired, but she heard every time Mark rolled over on his mattress.

"Mommy's here," she said, smoothing the dark hair back from his forehead. He grabbed her hand, clinging to it tightly. Sometimes he needed a shot, other times he settled down the minute she got there.

Being a heavy sleeper, Scott never heard Mark's cries. As Diane looked at his sleeping form, noticing the lighter hair fanning the pillow, she was thankful for his robust health. He was such a blessing. His appearance in the family was good. It helped give Mark a different perspective. Rather than being treated as an invalid, he was treated as one of the family. It helped him live as normal a life as possible.

Lisa Lyn Nason (the Lyn after Grandma Fehlman) was born on December 1, 1966, weighing seven pounds, eleven ounces. It was a difficult birth and the doctor had to use forceps.

Lisa was smaller at birth than her brothers had been. "Dainty like a girl should be," Dennis said.

Dr. Bill dropped by later. Grabbing Diane's hand, he walked with her down the hall toward the nursery.

"Well, we got our girl, didn't we?" he asked.

"She's a beauty," Diane said, pride showing in her smile.

Lisa's hair was sparse and dark. She looked like Dennis and his side of the family. Diane felt confident that Lisa would be healthy.

"It's going to be neat, having a girl to sew for," Diane told Dennis. "I can't wait to make her pretty, ruffly dresses. Maybe we'll have matching outfits."

Lisa was pure joy for Diane. She was a happy child. Her dark hair changed to a golden blond with highlights of red. She had fat cheeks and chubby little legs.

The Nasons began attending the same church as Diane's

parents. Now that Dennis had cut back on his extra jobs, he was home on Sundays, an answer to Diane's prayer. They started teaching a class in the Sunday school and felt they were again growing in the Lord. The Lord continued to shape and guide them every step of the way.

Many of the people in that church understood about Mark's problems and prayed for him on a daily basis. They also offered to help the busy young parents.

Diane enrolled Mark in school, but it didn't work out. When he wasn't home with asthma, he was in the hospital. From ages five to eight, Mark spent half of his life in the hospital. The Nasons paid for a tutor, as it was the only way Mark could keep up with his age group. It wasn't the best arrangement socially, as once again he was put into an adult world and developed most of his companionship with his tutors, parents and grandparents.

Lisa was six months old when Dennis and Diane again brought up the subject of adoption.

"It would be neat for Lisa to have a baby sister," Diane said. "I always wanted a sister when I was growing up."

The Nasons weren't thinking about more than one child at that point. They just wanted to round out the family to two boys and two girls. Yes, a girl *would* be nice to go with Lisa . . .

Chapter Three

The Celebration of Life Begins

Since the Nasons already had an "all-American family" with two boys and a girl, there were mixed reactions from friends and relatives when Dennis and Diane announced they were going to adopt.

Comments ranged from: "That's perfect. A sister will be nice for Lisa," to "It's great that you're giving a homeless baby a good home," to "*Why* would you want to adopt? Your family is the right size now," to "How can you adopt a child when you know nothing about the child's background?"

"It's just something we feel led to do," was Diane's pat answer.

"There are lots of kids who need homes, a family, someone to belong to," Dennis added. "We have a lot of love to offer and a good home to give a child."

"There's certainly a need, and we feel qualified to fill that need," Diane said.

"We talked about adopting kids before we were married," Dennis said.

"Even when you already have three of your own?" the question was inevitably asked.

"Yes, even though we have biological kids. That doesn't alter the need."

Diane didn't mention the problems of carrying and giving birth. That was nobody else's business. Adding to their family by adoption seemed like the best way.

The Nasons decided to go through the Children's Services Division that administered adoptions for the state of Oregon to apply for a baby girl. It was 1967, three years before the abortion law came into existence, and there were many babies available for adoption.

The first step of the process was the home study, a state requirement for each family considering adoption. The study consisted of the initial contact with the adoption agency, an interview in the office, followed by visits from a social worker to the home. After two or three visits, the worker determined whether or not the home was an adequate place for a child to live.

There were endless forms to be filled out, including medical and referral forms that were thoroughly investigated with friends and relatives. The medical forms required a physical for both husband and wife. The process wasn't difficult, but it was time consuming.

Because he was holding down two jobs, Dennis made enough to meet state income requirements and it looked good on paper.

The Nasons' decision to adopt was final. Lisa was only six months old, but Dennis and Diane figured it would be a long wait before a baby was available.

They submitted the application and met the caseworker, Ruth, for the first time.

Ruth fell in love with the family immediately and was enthusiastic about adoption for the Nasons.

"I have no qualms about recommending you for adoption. You are well prepared and seem to know what you're doing and what you want," Ruth said.

They weren't surprised at Ruth's comment. They knew they could handle another child. Because of Diane's efficiency and organizational abilities, an additional child would be no problem. More importantly, they had a lot of love to offer.

They expected a lengthy wait, but within six months, in January 1968, the call came.

"We just had a staff meeting and wanted to know if you would accept a baby girl who was born just a few weeks ago on December 20?"

Diane was so excited she could hardly speak. "I'll call Dennis, and get right back to you," she finally said.

"It's happened!" she cried when Dennis came to the phone.

"*What's* happened?"

"The baby girl. She's ready! Ruth just called."

"What are we waiting for?"

Diane laughed. "That's what I thought you'd say. I'll call Ruth and tell her yes."

"Of course we'll accept her," Diane blurted to Ruth. "No questions asked."

"Good," was Ruth's answer. "I'll set up an appointment for tomorrow. You can see a picture of the baby, and I'll give you all the information I have."

Diane could hardly sleep that night. They were going to adopt a baby. A little sister for Lisa. Lisa was thirteen months old and just learning to walk. They would grow up together, be great pals.

The next morning, which was Dennis's day off from the post office, he and Diane sat in Ruth's office, their faces glowing with anticipation.

"Well, here she is," Ruth said, handing Diane a picture of the baby. "This was taken by the foster mother."

A fat, chubby baby in an infant seat sat in front of a gaily decorated Christmas tree.

"Oh, Dennis, look at those chipmunk cheeks!" Diane cried. "Isn't she *beautiful?*"

Dennis nodded in agreement. It was love at first sight for the young couple. This was their baby. They both knew it. It was as if she had "Nason" printed on her forehead. "Oh, thank You, God," Diane murmured, reaching for Dennis's hand.

"We already have a name picked out," Diane said. "She's going to be Lori Diane."

"This little girl matches your family perfectly," Ruth said. "The mother's background is similar to yours, Diane."

"We don't care about that," Dennis said.

Ruth looked up from the sheath of papers she held in her hand. "I know, Dennis, but the state cares. We try to place babies with families by nationality, looks and interests."

It was uncanny, the Nasons agreed, that the baby's mother was the same height as Diane with long dark hair and brown eyes—and she loved horses.

"When can we see the baby?" Diane asked, not wanting to wait another day.

"As I already explained, these things take time," Ruth replied. "I'll set up an appointment for the meeting. How does the fifteenth of February sound?"

"February!" Diane exclaimed. "That's a whole month away."

Ruth shook her head. "I know it seems like a long time, but I can't make it any sooner. There are other babies scheduled to meet adoptive parents, so this is as soon as we can have a caseworker there."

"That settles it," Dennis said with a shrug. "Make it the fifteenth then."

The next four weeks seemed endless. Dennis and Diane

hated waiting. The procedure seemed pointless. Here was a baby who needed a home, and they were ready to provide that home. Why wait? Yet they knew the delay was mandatory—it was the way things worked.

Diane kept busy. Mark had another siege with asthma, Scott fell and cut his lip, and Lisa learned two new words.

February 15 finally arrived, and all five Nasons drove to the coastal town where the baby lived and checked into a motel. Lisa didn't understand what was happening, but Mark and Scott were excited.

"Are we really going to get a new baby?" Mark asked.

"You bet we are," Dennis said, leaning down and hugging his son. "A little girl named Lori."

"Why can't we get a boy?" Mark asked.

"We already have two boys," Diane said. "We need a girl."

An hour later they drove to the state office building and waited. Soon after they arrived, a lady walked in, holding a pink bundle in her arms.

"Here she is—"

Just as Diane reached out, the baby opened her eyes. "Oh, she's *beautiful*. Look at that smile," Diane exclaimed.

"And those dimples," Dennis added.

They took her back to the motel, laid her on the bed and unwrapped the blanket. She was perfectly formed from top to bottom. She smiled all the time, her big, brown eyes watching closely.

"Oh, Dennis," Diane cried, "it's just as if I gave birth to her with one exception—I feel terrific!"

Dennis peered down at the chubby face. "She's a Nason all right. I've never been more sure of anything." He frowned suddenly. "Can't we just take her home tonight?"

"Afraid not," Diane said. "You know the rules."

The procedure required the prospective parents to return

the child, go back home and talk it over, and to return the next morning if they still wanted the baby. That gave a couple the opportunity to change their minds.

But the Nasons knew, without a doubt, that Lori was to be theirs. So promptly at eight the next morning, they arrived to claim Lori Diane. Along with Lori they received a blanket, nightgown, and diary. The short-term foster mother had also written a four-page letter explaining the feeding schedule, among other bits of information. In part, her letter said:

> Your little pink bundle of joy was brought to us at three days of age. She was born December 20, 1967, and weighed eight pounds and four ounces. She was wrapped around our hearts from the beginning and at that tender age had already put her thumb in her mouth.

She concluded:

> Give our little doll lots of love and affection and she will more than reward you for it, and may God bless you and always take care of this little miracle from heaven, and may she bring the joy and happiness to you that she has brought to our home in the very short time we have been privileged to care for her for you.

Diane's eyes filled with tears. "Oh, Dennis, this is one wonderful foster mother. She loved Lori, and this diary is something Lori will treasure someday."

Mark, Scott and Lisa took to Lori right away.

"Baby!" Lisa said, standing on tiptoes to get a better look at the tiny infant in the crib.

"Yes, *baby*," Diane told her young daughter. "This is Lori, your baby sister. Someday you will play dolls with her. Won't that be fun?"

Now Diane had two babies in diapers, but she didn't mind. She liked keeping busy.

The Nasons soon discovered some people, even friends, found it very hard to accept adoption because both the heredity and environment of the child are unknown.

But Dennis and Diane responded on the basis of their faith. "We have faith that God chose this child for us. We just don't think that these traits are brought out in a child."

They felt it was their friends' problem because of their limited vision. The Nasons were learning already that they had to stay away from some families because of Mark's illness, and now they would be separating themselves in other ways because of adoption.

While Lisa was an indoor girl who preferred dolls and playing house, Lori was the opposite. She loved the outdoors, the rough and tumble, the horse and other animals.

A year after Lori's adoption, the Nasons moved back into town. Mark's asthma was worse and Dr. Bill suggested that living in town might help. "You'll be getting away from the various grasses and pollens. It might be what Mark needs."

Diane didn't like the idea, but was willing to try anything if it helped Mark. They bought a brand new house with the kind of carpet Mark needed, but it didn't help. Within months, Mark's asthma was worse.

In between the devastating asthma attacks, Diane tried to help Mark lead as normal a life as possible, but it was difficult. Diane signed up to be a Cub Scout den mother, and Dennis was Cubmaster, enabling Mark to take an active part when he was well, but that was not often the case.

"Why do I have to be like this?" he demanded. "I want to go to school! I don't *like* having tutors."

"I know, honey," Diane told her seven-year-old in sympathy. "I understand how you feel, but I don't have the answers. All I know is that God loves you, and I don't think He wants you to suffer. We just have to trust that God will help us find the answer. And maybe you'll be a better person for having gone through all this."

Diane managed to hold back the tears until she left his room. Then she broke down. *God, I don't understand either. He's a wonderful little person. He doesn't cry when he gets his shots, nor does he complain when he goes to the hospital, but he's tired of staying home from school.*

Dr. Bill came to the house on different occasions and took Mark bowling to give him an outside activity. Their bond strengthened, and it enriched Mark's life.

Mark had been put on cortisone months before, but still did not improve.

"I don't like increasing the cortisone, but looks like we'll have to do it," Dr. Bill said one day in his office.

"Is it really that harmful?" Diane asked.

"Yes," Dr. Bill answered. "If used over a long period of time, it can stunt growth, cause bone degeneration, and in some cases have a crippling effect."

The increased dosage didn't help, either. The cortisone made Mark's face swell to twice its size. It began affecting his personality, making him hostile toward Scott. On one occasion, he lit some matches and tried to start a fire. When disciplined, he cried, "Mommy, I don't know *why* I did that. I didn't mean to—"

"I know," Diane said, holding him close.

As Mark grew worse, Diane spent endless hours in the hospital. It wasn't unusual for Mark to be there for three weeks in a row. Sometimes Dennis would stay with the younger children, and sometimes Grandma or Grandpa stayed with them.

It was difficult to stand by while Mark grew weaker and failed to respond to medication. Diane had been giving

Mark adrenalin shots at home for a long time since they couldn't make it to the hospital, but the adrenalin didn't help, not even with increased dosage. Cortisone was the only medicine keeping Mark alive.

One day, during the worst attack Mark ever had, Dr. Bill issued a command: "Get Dennis over here quick! I don't know if Mark's going to make it!"

Dennis rushed into the hospital room ten minutes later to find Diane praying while Dr. Bill worked on Mark.

When the crisis had passed, Dr. Bill shook his head. "It wasn't me who pulled him out of this one. It was God."

Diane had never before heard Dr. Bill mention God in relation to Mark's illness. It was the first strengthening of Dr. Bill's walk with the Lord.

The Lord had pulled Mark through this time, but what about the next?

"I hate to say this," Dr. Bill told Dennis and Diane later, "But if Mark continues getting worse, he's not going to live past the age of nine."

For a brief moment, Diane felt her hope and faith wane. But she wasn't going to accept that prognosis. She couldn't. Besides, hadn't the Lord promised her that Mark would be all right—way back when he was first born—that he would go on to do great things? She had confidence in the Word of the Lord. Though she didn't understand the reason for Mark's suffering, she knew that God was in charge and leading every step of the way.

The Nasons finally left the hospital and headed for home, home where they would see normal, healthy kids—kids who could run and play, scream and holler without getting sick.

"I never thought the day would come when I'd feel so helpless, so scared," Dennis confided in Diane. "But, I *am* scared. We've got people praying at church, our friends in adoption, our families, and Mark isn't improving. What else can we do? *How can we stand by and watch our son die?"*

A few weeks later, Dr. Bill returned from a medical seminar at the Rusk Institute in New York. He had talked to another doctor about Mark's condition and was filled with sudden hope. He summoned the Nasons to his office.

"I think we've found the answer for Mark."

Dennis and Diane were stunned. "You *have*?" they said in unison.

Dr. Bill hesitated for a moment, knowing that what he was about to suggest would have a hard impact on the young couple. "There's a hospital for asthmatic children in Denver, Colorado. It's a residential, live-in situation. The exciting part is their excellent record for helping children like Mark."

Diane's face registered shock as she realized what Dr. Bill was saying. She looked at Dennis, then back at Dr. Bill. "You mean Mark would go there to live?"

Dr. Bill nodded. "Children have improved enough to be taken completely off cortisone. They learn how to pace themselves. They also get involved with physical therapy like swimming and bowling, and they learn to lead fairly normal lives for the first time—"

"But we can't move to Denver," Dennis broke in.

"That won't be necessary since Mark would live right at the hospital."

"But . . . that's so far away!" Diane sputtered.

"I know it's a big step," Dr. Bill continued, "but one I want you to give full consideration. Why not go home, discuss it, then let me know how you feel tomorrow?"

All Diane could think about was being away from Mark. *Mark would be gone a whole year.* How could she bear it? He'd been so much a part of her for the past eight years.

"I don't see how we can do it," Diane said to Dennis. "He might think we deserted him."

Dennis sighed. "I know, honey. That's how I feel too, but if it can help Mark, it's the only way."

After much prayer and deliberation, the Nasons agreed to send Mark to Denver. Their medical insurance would take care of expenses at the hospital, but the Nasons needed money for transportation. They had already obtained several loans to keep up with medical costs, and the church knew it. A love offering was taken one night and presented to Diane. The pastor phoned a church in Denver and made arrangements for Diane to stay with the Denver minister and his family. The minister also located a family, the Lemmons, who said they would pick up Mark each Sunday and take him to Sunday school and church. Everything was working out, and Diane began to feel her spirits rise.

The pastor met the airplane and drove Diane and Mark to the hospital. When he pulled up in front of the massive brick building, Diane panicked. *Oh, God, I can't do it. I can't leave Mark here.*

Grabbing Mark's hand, she went inside and met counselors, doctors, and other people involved with Mark's care. Once again, she felt encouraged. Children who couldn't even walk were in physical therapy, learning to swim and bowl. Mark looked excited.

"I'll be able to bowl, Mommy. And swim, too."

Diane was fine until the day she had to leave. *Lord,* she prayed, *how can I leave Mark? You're going to have to help me. Give me the strength to board that plane and go back to my family.*

The Lord seemed to speak to her. "You *can* do it, Diane. I'll help you. Lean on Me. One step at a time. One day at a time."

Diane returned to see Mark four times during that year, and each time it was nearly impossible to leave.

The year went by slowly, and Mark was almost ready to come home when the telephone rang one muggy July morning in 1970. It was Ruth, from the State Children's Services Division. "Diane, I have some great news! We have another baby girl for you. She's just three weeks old."

Diane had recently called Ruth, mentioning that she and Dennis would like to adopt again, but hadn't expected to hear this soon. Lori was already two and a half, and Diane missed having a baby in the house.

"This is the youngest baby we've ever put up for adoption," Ruth went on, "but this little girl needs a good home, and we know you two are just the ones to provide it."

"I really feel the Lord is leading us in this adoption," Diane said when she called Dennis at work. "It's like we need something good and positive happening in our lives now."

"I agree," Dennis answered. "Call Ruth back and tell her to get the papers started."

The baby was in Portland. This time they wouldn't have to wait two months to see her. She was ready *now.*

"I can't believe this," Diane said as they headed for Portland.

The kids jumped up and down in the back seat. "We're getting a new baby!" Scott yelled.

"That's right," Diane said, looking back at her three children. The only thing marring this celebration was Mark's absence.

They had left so suddenly, they hadn't told Diane's parents, who were away on a camping trip. Nobody but Ruth knew that they were going to pick up a baby.

They located the Portland address and took the kids with them when they went in to see the baby.

The girl in the office looked at Diane strangely. "You're adopting?" she asked, looking from Diane to Dennis, then over at Scott, Lisa and Lori. "Looks like you have a nice-sized family already."

"We like to adopt," Diane said, feeling a bit foolish. She didn't care to explain how they felt led by God to adopt again. Besides, an explanation wasn't necessary. It was their business and the Lord's.

"The baby will be out in a few minutes," the girl said.

They waited about thirty minutes. Suddenly a baby wrapped in a white blanket was placed in Diane's arms.

Lifting back the blanket, they stared in amazement.

"Oh, Dennis, isn't she exquisite?"

She had black curly hair, huge, bright blue eyes, a tiny turned-up nose, and a dimple in her chin.

"Thank You, Lord, just thank You," was all Dennis could say.

The little ones flocked around and looked at the sleeping baby.

"Baby, see the baby," Lori said excitedly.

"I *like* this baby," Lisa said, clapping her hands.

"Is she really a girl?" Scott asked, stepping out of his untied sneaker.

"Well, yes, son, that's right," Dennis said. "But girls are nice. Don't you like your sisters?"

Scott wrinkled his nose. "They're okay sometimes, but I wish Mark was here."

"So do I, Scott," Diane said under her breath.

They returned to the motel room they had rented for the night. "I suppose we have to wait until morning to take her home," Dennis said.

"You know the procedure," Diane answered. She wondered how anyone could give up this baby. She was so perfect.

As they drove toward home the next morning Diane had

an idea. "Let's go by Indian Mary Campground where Mom and Dad are and show them their new granddaughter."

"Good idea," Dennis said. "Won't they be surprised?"

To say the Fehlmans were surprised is an understatement. As Diane walked over to the picnic table with the bundle in her arms, her mother looked up. The children ran ahead and surrounded their grandparents with shouts and happy whoops. "We've got a new baby! We've got a new baby!"

"Why, Diane, I had no idea you were going to adopt again!" her mother said.

Diane laughed. "Well, it was sudden. The call came after you and Dad left, and we went right on up to Portland and picked her up. No waiting like with Lori."

"She's the most precious little girl you ever saw," Dennis said.

"What're you going to call her?" Don Fehlman asked, peering inside the white blanket. As if on cue, the baby opened her eyes and seemed to study the faces looking at her.

"Katie," Diane said. "Katie Sue. The people who take Mark to church in Denver have a little girl, and her name is Katie Sue. It really fits!"

"I like the name," her father said.

Katie did everything early. She laughed at three weeks, walked and ran by the time she was nine months old. She was high-strung, got into everything, and was hard to scold since she would laugh and run away. Everything was a big joke to Katie.

"I know why God led us to Katie Sue so early in her life," Diane said to Dennis one morning.

"Why is that?" he asked.

"Because no one could jump in midstream and catch up

with her. It's a good thing she arrived at three weeks, because we've been able to grow with her."

Katie Sue had been with her new family two weeks when the call came from Denver. Mark was ready to come home!

Diane was ecstatic. "We'll have a big dinner and ask Mom and Dad over. I'll make Mark's favorite meal. You know how he loves hamburgers and lemon cake."

"I'll make a big banner saying, Welcome Home, Mark," Dennis offered.

After a trip to the Medford Airport to pick up Mark, followed by many hugs and kisses, the Nasons went home to celebrate. Diane was relieved to have her whole family together again. But it didn't seem the same; Mark had changed drastically.

"He's so thin," Diane said.

"It's his attitude that worries me," Dennis added. "He's sullen."

"And aloof," Diane said. "As if he doesn't dare depend on anyone."

"They probably taught him to be self-sufficient at the hospital," Dennis said.

"I wish we had the old Mark back. I could talk to him before—about everything. We were so close." Diane shook her head. "It hurts to see him like this."

"He'll come around," Dennis said. "It'll just take time. We have to be patient."

Still, Diane worried. How could she tell her son that they had never stopped loving him—that they left him in the hospital in hopes of his getting well?

In fact, Mark was far from well. He continued to be in and out of the hospital. He had serious colds, pneumonia, and required oxygen and intravenous feeding on occasion.

"That whole year was wasted," Diane complained to Dr.

Bill three weeks later. "Here he is, being rushed to the hospital, struggling for every breath."

Dr. Bill was sympathetic. "I know how you feel, Diane. But keep in mind that we did what we set out to do—we got him off the cortisone."

Diane knew Dr. Bill was right. She knew, too, that the main reason she felt anger was because she missed Mark's love and companionship. If only he hadn't changed. Maybe she could think of something to cheer him up. And then the idea came.

"I know a pet we can get Mark," Diane said the next morning at the breakfast table.

As all eyes turned in her direction, Diane blurted out, "An iguana."

"Iguana?" Dennis questioned. "You mean one of those ugly looking toads?"

"No, it's a lizard—an American lizard."

"*Lizard?*" Dennis's face turned pale. "A lizard is like a snake, and you know how I feel about snakes—"

"But, it's the only kind of pet Mark can have," Diane said. "No hair, no fur or feathers. It's just the ticket."

It wasn't a cuddly pet, but it belonged to Mark and that made it special. The iguana was part of the Nason household for over a year, and everyone learned to enjoy José.

Dr. Bill kept searching for new ways, new people who could help Mark. His careful inquiry led to Dr. Deamer of the University of California Medical School in San Francisco.

"Yes, I'd like to meet this boy and see if we can help him," Dr. Deamer said. "We're doing great things in research now for severe asthmatics."

Deamer and his associates had done follow-up studies on several kids from the Denver hospital, realizing it doesn't do any good to remove a child from an unhealthy atmosphere, and then put him back in the same atmosphere and expect him to be one hundred percent better.

Dr. Bill made the contact with Dr. Deamer, and soon the Nasons were on their way to San Francisco.

Dr. Deamer, a man of about seventy, still had dark hair and flashing eyes. "I hope you don't think I'm going to cure your son," he said.

Dennis and Diane were taken aback. Of course they were looking for a cure. That is what they had prayed for—that Mark could be helped permanently.

"We hope you can at least *help* Mark," Dennis finally said.

"What we need to do is pray, and pray now. *God* is the one who is going to help your boy."

Oh, Lord, thank You, Diane thought. *A Christian doctor. It's more than we dared hope for.*

"I suppose you've had all kinds of skin testing done," the doctor began.

"Yes, many, many times."

"I hope you know they're totally invalid for food."

No, they hadn't known.

"I want you to start an elimination diet right away, then next month when you come down—"

"*Next month?*" Dennis broke in.

"Yes, I expect you to come in every month."

Another upheaval. It was a long, hard trip. From Ashland to San Francisco was about four hundred miles. It would be hard financially, but the Lord had led them this far—surely He would provide the necessary funds. Staying with relatives on the way down helped with the lodging expense. Dr. Bill gave them the name of a hotel close to the hospital that was reasonable.

Every month they made the long trip. The Nasons got to know San Francisco as well as they had Denver—the zoo, parks, museums and other spots.

The elimination diet was difficult. Diane had to take away all foods, give a few back, then start all over again if a reaction resulted. Mark didn't like the diet, but he went along with it. "If this is something I have to do, let's get on with it," he said.

"Dr. Deamer thinks it will help," Dennis said, putting an arm around his son.

During these trips to see Dr. Deamer, a big breakthrough in allergy medications was announced. It was called IN-TAL, and best of all, there were no side effects. INTAL was a powder prescribed in capsule form. It kept allergens (substances that cause allergies) from coming into the system and thus eliminated the cause of the attack. However, the drug was only available from England and Canada, and it was expensive to import: three hundred dollars a shipment.

Dr. Bill knew a friend in Canada who sent some down. The friend knew about the Nasons and offered it for one hundred dollars. But even that was too much for the Nasons. "It may as well be a thousand," Diane said, despair in her voice.

"Let's give it to the Lord," Dennis said, "just like we've always done. We have to keep on, one day at a time, like He's taught us."

The money came in through an unexpected source—an anonymous donor.

Dr. Deamer worked with the INTAL and the diet, and Mark was able to come out of his severe asthmatic state and start leading a normal existence for the first time in his life. He could even go outside and help with the laying hens.

"You'd better keep him away from horses and furry animals, but let's see how he does with the chickens," Dr. Bill said.

Mark was ecstatic. "I'm going to sell these eggs to Grandma," he declared, holding up a full basket he'd just gathered.

Mark Andrew Nason, now twelve years old, was finally going to school for the first time on a permanent basis. What a long, winding path Mark had come down! But the Lord had been with him all the way—watching, protecting, guiding.

Dennis and Diane had been growing, too. Learning to trust, learning to accept, they had discovered they could handle just about any handicap or illness. And they could provide a loving home for children who had none.

Chapter Four

The Vietnamese Connection

It was 1972, and the United States was at war in Vietnam, one of the most unpopular wars in our history. Many people thought we were doing the right thing by sending our boys to help preserve freedom for the South Vietnamese. Others thought we had no business fighting in that situation. It was an emotional time.

The Nasons had a different reason for being disappointed in our involvement. They were concerned for the hundreds of fatherless babies in Vietnam. Babies with either United States fathers who had returned home or Vietnamese fathers who had lost their lives in battle were rejected by the Vietnamese.

"There's one thing we can do, and that is to help these children," Diane told Dennis. "I've prayed that somehow a door will be opened to let us help in some way."

"And how could we do that?" Dennis asked.

"I believe we should adopt a child," Diane answered. "A child injured in a war that he had no part in."

"But I don't see how," Dennis said.

Diane thrust the magazine section from the Sunday paper toward Dennis. "This article tells about a Vicky Galvin from New York who's working with a lady involved in adoptions in Vietnam. It says this is one of the first attempts at adopting Amerasian and Vietnamese children."

"But this Vicky's in New York, and we're in Oregon," Dennis said. "How will we contact her?"

"The name of her street is here, although no number," Diane said. "I'll write, then sit back and wait for an answer. I know the Lord can deliver this letter."

"You never cease to amaze me," Dennis said with a hug.

"Dennis, these are helpless children we're talking about. If we turn our back on them, who is going to help?"

"No one, I suppose."

"You know we applied for a handicapped child through the state more than a year ago," Diane went on. "I can't believe they don't have any to place, but that's what they say. Maybe the Lord is leading us in another direction—to become involved in the lives of the Vietnamese children."

Diane wrote to Vicky. "Lord, if You want us to work with the children there, help this letter to reach the right person," she prayed.

A month later Diane received an answer.

"I am interested in talking with you," the letter said. "Enclosed are names of people to contact. I am working with Rosemary Taylor and helping to set up key people around the United States who believe as we do." Rosemary Taylor, a young Australian who was teaching in an American school, had gone to Vietnam and was appalled at the plight of the children there. She set up orphanages, but found that red tape made adoptions extremely difficult. Rosemary cared for the children while trying to break down those barriers.

Diane was given the name of a woman with the Red

Cross in Da Nang, who was deeply involved in finding means by which these children could be adopted. Diane wrote to her in September 1972.

> We have five children, of which two are adopted. We feel God is leading us to help children in Vietnam. We want a child who has been injured in the war. We feel strongly about that, and think we can handle just about any problem.

They thought it would be months before they received an answer, but it was dated November 2—Dennis's birthday:

> I discussed your letter with Miss Yvonne Santag, director of the China Beach Protestant Orphanage, which is sponsored by United World Mission. She had all the information about you and discussed it with her fellow missionaries. Well, after talking it over, she has decided to offer you little Tam, a three-year-old child. The girl is handicapped and will require operations to reset her hand, which is twisted out of shape at the wrist. The operation will need to be done in the States.
>
> You will like little Tam. She is so lovable and so sweet that you and your children will know what a wonderful gift God has given to you. I know you can bring a great deal of happiness into her life, just as she will bring happiness into yours.

Another letter arrived from China Beach Orphanage on November 8.

> I am a nurse and handle adoption requests we receive here at China Beach. We don't participate in adoptions much, as we do not have a sufficient staff to handle the necessary paperwork. Most of the three hundred children are older and have siblings. Enclosed you'll find a picture of our little Tam.

The picture showed a tiny girl with black, short hair, and a big, bright smile.

"Oh, Dennis, isn't she perfect?" Diane cried. "I don't even notice any scars or deformities—"

"She's a cutie, all right," Dennis said in agreement. "What do we do now?"

Diane wrote immediately. "She's our child—we both know it. What comes next?"

Thus began the long siege of paperwork.

This adoption would be handled by the Immigration and Naturalization Service which asks that a local agency investigate the adoption. The Nasons looked to their friend Ruth at the state agency for support.

"My superiors don't understand, but I believe in what you're doing," she said.

Usually a home study is not required for an overseas private adoption, but the state of Oregon required another home study and the Nasons wanted to be completely aboveboard.

That decision started a long line of communication with China Beach and the Red Cross worker, who was handling the paperwork for the Nasons.

Diane wrote, telling the name they had chosen for little Tam. Kari Marie. Marie for Dennis's grandmother who loved children, and for Marie Prescott, who had taught both Dennis and Scott in the first grade at the same school in Ashland. Marie Prescott had devoted her entire life to teaching children.

"Kari Marie is learning her new name," was the next response from the orphanage. "She can also say 'please, thank you, I love you, and Mom and Dad.' We tried to explain about you, but she doesn't understand."

Marsha, an American nurse who cared for Kari at the Hoa Khaun Children's Hospital, wrote about Kari's background.

Kari is from the Hue area, north of Da Nang. The scars on her face and body were caused by burns from a gasoline fire. She was treated in a hospital near her home but developed severe contractures of both hands. The burns on her arms and hands were caused by a napalm explosion. The doctors tried to correct one hand, but due to infection, the correction was not completed. Little Tam was brought to the Hoa Khaun Children's Hospital on July 30, 1972. We have not heard from any of her family.

We will continue praying that papers will be completed soon, so that she may be with her new family. Be prepared to wait several months, as we do not have a birth certificate for her yet.

It was now December 1972.

"Kari's one of the fortunate ones," Diane told Dennis. "Because of her handicap, she is being cared for in good, clean surroundings in a hospital. Most of the children are in the streets and dying of malnutrition."

On January 22, 1973, the Nasons received a letter from another person in Kari's life. Micki McCrary had recently returned to the States after working for a year as secretary and general assistant at the Hoa Khaun Children's Hospital.

Marsha wrote me, telling me that our little Tam was to be adopted. I decided to write. One of the saddest things about leaving Vietnam was my fear that Kari Marie would be swallowed up by the type of life so many Vietnamese children live. Kari is such a bright, cheerful, happy child. I am enclosing extra copies of pictures I have of her. Her personality and abilities were so wonderful to me that I seldom thought of the deformities. If you have any questions, or if there is any way I can help, please feel free to ask.

Micki made copies of eighty of her slides and sent them to Dennis and Diane as a present for Kari.

"What a legacy," Diane exclaimed. "These slides tell of Kari's heritage and are something she will cherish always."

The slides had a twofold purpose. Diane had copies made that were sent to schools and shown to people who wanted to help. The slides told better than words the work that was needed with the Vietnamese children. The Nasons felt the Lord had picked Kari to be theirs, so the slides could spread the needs of thousands of orphans.

In April another letter came from China Beach Orphanage, thanking Diane for the cards and letters. Diane had sent pictures of the family so Kari could get acquainted with her family-to-be.

> The Lord continues to provide for our many needs. There are fewer American products available, but we are receiving powdered milk and flour to supplement the children's diet. In many ways the children were spoiled by the troops, and it became a habit to expect a handful of goodies without being grateful.
>
> Kari's in good health. She has the usual number of colds, cuts, and bruises, and occasionally needs a penicillin shot to help clear up infected insect bites, which are quite common here. It was noticed by a coworker that Kari's eyes don't focus on things she is looking at. Perhaps corrective lenses will be needed. Just thought it best to let you know.

The birth certificate which the Nasons had applied for in December 1972 arrived in April. Immigraton would not give approval until after they received the birth certificate. The approval came in June 1973. The Immigration and Naturalization Service had cabled the American consul in Saigon, and the home study was used to verify that all state requirements had been met. The Nasons knew that soon their beautiful little girl would arrive.

However, Immigration was not satisfied. A letter arrived, voicing their objections. In part it read:

According to the report of overseas orphan investigation concerning Hoang Thi Tam (the whole name they attached to the birth certificate), the child has deformed hands due to burns and also scars on her legs, abdomen, and face. Please advise by return mail if you still wish to proceed with the adoption in view of this additional information.

"Yes, bureaucracy or not, that is the one reason that Kari Marie is coming," Diane and Dennis replied. "Already she has been a source of inspiration to thousands of Americans. Because of a war that severely handicapped her, she has been able to reach hundreds of people and tell them of the needs of these children just like her."

Because the orphanages and their staffs were supported entirely by donations from Americans, various drives were set up in leading American cities. There were several chapters throughout the United States, with headquarters in Denver, Colorado. Diane was the logical one to head up the unit in southern Oregon, and she soon became the northwest coordinator.

"People have to be made aware of the plight of these youngsters," Diane told friends. "While we wait for children to be adopted, many things can be done. Christian people need to realize they are responsible for the children of the world."

While waiting for Kari to "come home," Diane was encouraged by the response of others. Doctors sent free medicine, hundreds of people gathered boxes of clothing and nonperishable food items, while others were busy getting the parcels in the mail.

Diane continued traveling everywhere, showing Kari's slides, and receiving donations from different groups who viewed the slides. People signed pledges to help support a baby or an older child. Another fundraising project was a cookbook that included recipes Diane collected from friends and acquaintances. Poems by Vietnamese writers were also included, along with pictures of the children, their big brown eyes full of expression and bewilderment. The cookbook was a huge success.

Finally, on January 8, 1974, a full year from the time the initial inquiry was made, Kari Marie Nason arrived at the San Francisco Airport. Dennis and Diane and the children all drove down for the great occasion.

They dashed off to the terminal, afraid they might be late. Diane hurried toward the gate, with everyone in close pursuit. The plane was completely unloaded—but no Kari Marie.

Diane stopped the first person she saw with an airport nametag.

"We were supposed to meet our little girl from Vietnam," she began explaining.

"Oh, yes. Those children were taken directly to customs," he said, pointing down a long hall.

Suddenly Mark came running around the corner. He had gone off on his own, looking for Kari.

"I found her—I know it's her! She's with a stewardess."

There she was, little Kari Marie, looking like a china doll, barely twenty-two pounds at four years of age, and so afraid. She was dressed in a lovely *ai dai*, the national dress of the Vietnamese women. The staff at the orphanage had chosen it especially for her trip home.

Kari spoke no English, and she looked from Dennis to Diane with large, round, black eyes.

Diane reached out and wrapped her in her arms. She didn't speak, but Kari sensed that this was home and this was her new "mama."

Her real homecoming came the next day. Kari smiled as she entered each room of the Nason house. The bathroom intrigued her, as she wasn't used to toilets. That night when

Diane tucked her into her new bed, she smiled again, then promptly fell asleep.

In the days that followed, the Nasons discovered their new adopted daughter had a mind of her own. They took her to see Dr. Bill immediately. He ran blood tests and X-rays, and she protested loudly. Every time he touched her she recoiled, watching him with terror-stricken eyes.

"Don't worry about her reaction," Dr. Bill said to Diane. "I imagine she's known a lot of doctors and pain in her short life. She needs immediate surgery on her hand. I'll recommend a reconstructive surgeon."

The first surgery was performed three months after Kari's arrival. The nurses were prepared for a traumatic time in the hospital, but Kari came through it with no problem. She took everything in stride—even the painful skin grafts were tolerated with only a flicker of pain in her eyes. Kari's face and arms required six operations before it was over.

The first five months after Kari's arrival, she seemed to adjust with no difficulty. She ate everything in sight, lost her fear of farm animals, slept well, and was a model child.

Then she rebelled for no apparent reason. Suddenly, Kari refused to eat, wet her bed, and became overly dependent on Diane. But then another change—when she discovered that neither Dennis nor Diane would bend to her many whims and that she was no different from her brothers and sisters, Kari made the transition back to obedience and became an enthusiastic member of the family.

"Some of the stubbornness is still there," Diane said to Dennis one evening after the children were in bed, "but I keep reminding myself that it was this same stubbornness and determination that kept her alive in Vietnam."

In April, the Nasons received a letter from Marie Prescott, the teacher who was one of Kari's namesakes.

Of all of the lovely things, including the love and friendship that you have sent my way, the greatest is the love you have shown in letting your little new daughter carry my name. The name itself is not important, but that you include me in the love you have for Kari Marie is more precious to me than I have words to express. Bless you, each one, for the loveliest Easter gift anyone ever had. Of course, I want to hear all about Kari Marie and meet her when she gets home. Please give each of your children a big hug and kiss for me. Are you aware what you are doing for your family as they grow up with their hearts open to accept always another member of the family or another friend? All of you are an inspiration to the rest of us. Thank you for your precious love.

After Kari's arrival and the adjustment period, Diane began thinking about adopting another child. Adopting directly from an orphanage in Vietnam was no longer possible; only agency adoptions were legal. Everything went through the state, and Diane knew there would be problems. Hadn't the state already said they couldn't possibly provide adequately for more than eight children? Wouldn't they balk more than ever? Still, Diane went to Ruth and told her she needed help in bringing another child home, a Vietnamese sister for Kari.

Ruth shook her head. "I'll be sticking my neck out, but I'll do it. However, this is the last time, Diane. You'll have to get someone else to work with you on the home study. I just can't do it anymore."

There were objections, but the home study was conducted. Then came another long wait.

Kecia Ruth—named Ruth after the one who had helped the Nasons so much—was eight months old and weighed a mere eight pounds when she arrived in San Francisco in August 1974.

Kecia Ruth arrived with her head covered with boils. Her hair was falling out because of infection, her tummy was bloated, and her arms and legs were spindles.

As Diane walked to the back of the jumbo jet where the children sat, she could only see one: Kecia. Kecia was strapped in a seat by herself, just sitting there. When their eyes met, Diane lost her breath, and at that moment, the closeness and bonding started. Kecia's eyes reflected the pain, horror, and utter hopelessness of a baby suffering from severe malnutrition—an unforgettable look.

For the special announcement of Kecia's arrival, Diane chose some fitting lines from "Fate" by Susan Marr Spalding:

Two shall be born the whole wide world apart;
And speak in different tongues, and have no thought
Each of the other's being, and no heed;
And these o'er unknown seas to unknown lands
Shall cross, escaping wreck, defying death,
And all unconsciously shape every act
And bend each wandering step to this one end,
That, one day, out of darkness, they shall meet
And read life's meaning in each other's eyes.

Five other children arrived on the same overseas flight, and Kecia was the youngest.

"I can't stand to think of her being so sick," Diane said.

"And think of the thousands more like her," Dennis added.

The Nasons decided to stop off at Norma and Ken Lucas's, friends in adoption, to show them Kecia.

Norma looked alarmed. "I'll certainly be praying for this little one," she said.

Her prayers were needed. A few days later, Kecia started running a fever. Diane rushed her to see Dr. Bill, and he immediately ran every test he knew about. There were no parasites or worms in the stomach or intestinal tract. All the strange maladies that came out of warm, humid Vietnam were discounted.

"But what can be wrong?" Diane cried, not daring to think that something could happen to Kecia. "Lord," she prayed, "You didn't give us Kecia to let her come home to die. Please help us locate the problem."

Then Diane thought about calling the orphanage. It was a trans-Pacific call, but Diane had to try. "Are any of the children sick?" she asked the director.

"Oh, my, yes," the director answered. "We lost ten babies last week, all from Kecia's section."

"What was wrong?" Diane asked, knowing she had to know, yet afraid of the answer.

"The hard measles," came the reply.

"Oh, thank you," Diane cried, hanging up the phone. She relayed the news to Dr. Bill.

"Now that we know what we're dealing with, it's easier, but we still have no guarantee that she'll pull through, Diane," Dr. Bill said. "Measles is bad enough, without all the other things she has to fight."

Twelve hours later, Kecia broke out in a rash that covered her tiny body. She went down to six pounds, and was hospitalized, fighting for her life. The tiny, defenseless Vietnamese baby who had known nothing but pain and hunger for all her short life was added to the prayer list of many people.

The prayers were answered, and soon the tiny little girl came home. She began gaining weight, and a sparkle came to her big, brown eyes. She had made it through the crisis.

Diane felt moved to record on paper how she felt about Kecia, and the Lord inspired Diane to write a letter to Kecia's birth mother, a woman she would never know. It was a letter to help Kecia understand the war she had no part in, and Diane's thoughts about becoming Kecia's mother.

LETTER TO AN UNKNOWN MOTHER

I don't think of you very often. In fact, most of the time I make an effort to keep you out of my thoughts. And yet . . . sometimes . . . just before I drift off to sleep or when I look into my daughter's eyes, I think of you.

I don't know you. Are you a woman? A girl of 16? There are so many reasons why you might have chosen to give up your baby (now so very much *our* baby). Was it the war, hunger, the realization that you could not provide even the most meager existence for her? Your husband's death? It must have been a terribly difficult decision and even harder to live through such an experience. I feel so sad for you, because it is sad to create something so lovely and then to be forced to turn your back on it. You must have felt some love too, if not for the baby, perhaps for her father. It is true you bore my daughter, but I am now her mother. I love her, "mother" her, live with her, care for her. Surely you must wonder about me. I'd like you to know how very much we love our daughter and how grateful we are to you for being the life force that brought her into being. Thank you for giving her her big black eyes, her soft skin, her happy beautiful spirit, her bright mind. Thank you for giving us this child who is everything we had ever hoped.

As time goes by, we will think of each other less and less. You are starting your life anew, and hopefully you will have another chance to gain happiness.

We are finding fulfillment for our lives in our daughter. But now, while you are still very much on my mind, I want to say "Thank you."

The work continued and hundreds of orphans were brought out of the war-torn country, but many remained there. Diane continued to show Kari's slides and speak throughout Oregon. She also worked on legislation with Senator Mark Hatfield of Oregon to ease the red tape in the adoption process. She prayed, along with countless others, that more people would respond to the need. Many did. But some waited too long, and when they finally decided to take a child, it was too late.

For most Americans the end of the Vietnam war brought a sense of relief. But for the Nasons the news was tragic. Yes, the war was over, but Vietnam had fallen to the Communists, and with it went the orphanages and the future of hundreds of children.

Diane and other coworkers cried bitter tears for those children who would never know freedom in America, never know the warm embrace of a family who cared. For them it was too late.

Chapter Five

Why Adopt?

---

*W*hy *would anyone want to adopt if they already have biological children?*

How can you consider adopting a physically handicapped child?

What? Adopt a racially mixed child? A Cambodian baby? Why would I want to do that?

No way, not me. If I adopt, it has to be a white kid. White with blond hair and blue eyes. It's got to look like my side of the family.

Sure, I know kids have special needs, but let someone else worry about them. I'm too busy.

Why adopt? Why not take in foster children? Then the state pays for their care.

The Nasons hear these comments often. Does it bother them?

"Not anymore," Diane said. "These are God's children. Everyone has something to put up with. Fat or thin, cerebral-palsied or armless, slow or clumsy, no one is perfect. But some day all the handicaps will be taken away. In heaven there will be no imperfections. Our job is to help all these children reach their highest potential, whatever it may be, and to grow with the Lord as their guide."

Why have the Nasons adopted so many children? Why didn't they choose to provide foster care instead?

"We don't believe in foster care, except in short-term cases," Diane said. "We want the children to belong to us. We want to give them our name, to be entirely responsible for their care. We want to offer a permanency to their lives—a feeling of belonging—something long-term foster care doesn't give."

Adoptive parents are committed to the premise that all waiting children have a right to a "forever family" in which each child can find nurturing, loving, and permanent parents.

"I believe there is a valid place for short-term foster care, such as in Lori's case," Diane said. "That foster mother took Lori, knowing that an adoptive home would be found. In the meantime, she cared for Lori as if she were her own and lovingly recorded her progress. That diary is something Lori will always cherish."

"But there are foster parents," Diane continued, "who take in children because of the money received for their care. In that kind of environment kids 'know' and grow up with a chip on their shoulder. They want to belong to a family. They *need* to belong."

Diane and Dennis believe the Lord started them on a step-by-step adoption program using Lori as a model. She was an example as more children arrived. Diane and Dennis grew in their knowledge and abilities as their family grew.

An adopted child looks for an identity with his or her parents. "Everyone wants to be wanted and to be able to relate to their parents in either looks or actions," Diane said. "It's just an automatic thing with children."

Another minus for foster care is lack of control. "Unless

you're totally in charge of a child, especially an older child, there are usually outside influences, influences you want to keep away from the child," Diane said.

The disappointments the Nasons have experienced have resulted from children caught in the foster care system too long. These children cannot cope or change. They can't believe that their adoptive home is permanent, that someone really cares. After ten or twelve years of foster care, they may be adopted by a family who loves and wants what is best for them, but often it's too late. The nights of crying into their pillows and asking, "Why can't I be adopted?" are repressed. These children become unreachable.

In other cases, a child wants to be adopted, but the biological family will not give him or her up. They want to keep that one last tie, though they may never plan to have the child live with them. There is something in their minds that will not let them cut that tie, even when they know it is best for their child.

Bill was a product of the foster care system. He had been in and out of foster homes all his life. He had a mother and nearly a dozen brothers and sisters, with all but the youngest in foster homes.

When the Nasons were first approached about taking Bill, Diane was adamant. "We only adopt. We don't believe in long-term foster care."

"The mother won't sign the papers."

Bill was fourteen and ill with asthma. He had gone to Children's Hospital in Denver shortly after Mark. The state knew that if anyone could handle Bill and his problem, Diane could.

"If you don't take him, he'll be institutionalized. He's too sick for most foster parents to cope with."

Neither Dennis nor Diane wanted to see Bill kept in an

institution, so after much discussion and lots of prayer, they agreed to take him.

The Nasons were surprised when Bill arrived in January 1971 with the social worker. He was a small boy for fourteen, not even topping five feet. Besides being small for his age, due to his struggle with asthma and his dependency on cortisone, Bill had emotional problems. Since he'd never had a father, Dennis became the father figure Bill had craved. He saw his mother only once or twice a year, but because he knew her, it was harder for him to accept Diane as his mother.

"Diane may not be your mom," Dennis explained, putting an arm around Bill's shoulder, "but you must show her respect and since all the other kids call her Mom, I feel that you should too."

Bill was good company for Mark. Since both were limited in their physical activities, they built models and played games together.

Several of Bill's brothers, who were a bad influence, tried to visit Bill. "But we couldn't have them at the house," Diane said. "It wasn't good to subject the little kids to that sort of behavior. Finally, I spoke to the social worker, who was cooperative."

The visits were disturbing for Bill. Since he was highstrung like most allergic children, it didn't take much to trigger an attack. Bill's brothers quit coming to the house, but they would stop off at school and see him there. They continued to be an outside force that pulled him one way— in the wrong direction.

Bill accepted the Lord not long after he came to live with the Nasons. "We'll always be thankful we were able to introduce him to the Lord," Diane said.

He became a part of the family as much as possible, even using the Nason name.

"I want to be adopted," Bill told Dennis frequently.

"I know, Bill," Dennis said with a sigh, "but it just isn't possible. When you reach eighteen, if you still want to be our legally adopted son, then you can."

Bill had his good days and his bad. He didn't like school, except for woodworking, but he enjoyed 4-H activities and took an active interest in computer technology.

Still, his brothers kept pulling him in another direction. Under their influence, he had started smoking, an especially bad habit for an asthmatic. In the end, the Nasons had no real parental control. "He wasn't ours, and he knew that he wasn't," Diane said.

"Bill," Dennis said, "you've only got three months left until graduation, and Dr. Bill still wants to help train you to give others inhalant therapy. You've got to hang in there."

Bill's grades were up, and the Nasons had made sure that he would be able to graduate. It seemed there was no possible way he could foul up his graduation, but he left in April.

The note Diane found said:

Dear Mom and Dad,

This is the last time I'll be able to call you Mom and Dad. I don't know what's wrong with me. I don't care what I'm doing half the time. I can't really control myself. I don't want to hurt anyone, especially you. I've got to go. Please don't try to find me.

Dennis and Diane cried. "So much beautiful potential—potential for the Lord," Diane said. "He's just going to be dragged through the gutter, and it isn't even his fault. *Why* didn't his mother let him be adopted? *Why* wouldn't his brothers leave him alone?"

Friends on the police force told Dennis they had picked

Bill up, finding him strung out on drugs. Once he was on a park bench, another time under a bridge.

Dennis went down to the jail several times and prayed with Bill. Diane sent some personal items and the picture album so he would remember "his family."

Later Bill left the area, because he would have been in jail permanently if he had stayed in Ashland.

Bill's presence in their home gave the Nasons a bitter taste of foster care and what can happen because of a lack of permanency in a child's life. It made them even more aware of how important adoption is to children of all ages.

Herbert Hansen, program director of Albertina Kerr Center for Children in Portland, Oregon, says:

> We want to encourage people to adopt, but first they must ask themselves a few questions: How is their marriage? Are they *both* eager about adopting? Will they be secure as parents? Would they accept children with handicaps? There will be a lot of changes in the family; some of them can be quite disruptive. The parents must be loving and patient, able to set limits, firm, but understanding. They must accept the child where he is. Any age child needs to feel he is special. He needs time to adjust and to become part of the family.
>
> We look at each child and try to determine the need. Our goal is for all children to have a permanent home in which to grow up, to be secure. Adoption is the superior way to achieve that.

"Commitment is the key word," Diane says. "Commitment never to quit helping the child, praying for the child, seeking the advice of other parents and professionals, if needed—and commitment to the Lord, to raise that child for however long He asks you to be an intricate part of his or her life."

Not flesh of my flesh nor bone of my bone,
but still miraculously my own.
Don't forget for a single minute, you didn't
grow under my heart but in it.

Anonymous

Chapter Six

The Biracial Child

We did not plant you, true.
But when the season is done,
when the alternate prayers for sun
and rain are counted,
when the pain of weeding and the
pride of watching you through,
then we will hold you high,
shining sheaves above the thousand
seeds grown tall.
Not our planting, but, by heaven,
our harvest, our children.
Anonymous

Some remarks by an acquaintance of the Nasons represent the viewpoint of many people in today's society. Shortly after the Nasons moved to Sisters, this man asked Dennis where on earth all those kids had come from.

"Why, they're mine," Dennis said proudly.

The man looked shocked. "Well, I'll tell you one thing: I can't stand niggers or slants."

"That's your problem," Dennis said, walking off.

Biracials are finding more acceptance now compared to a few decades ago. There have always been Indian/white children. Later, following World War II, there were many Oriental/white, and, more recently, black/white. Still, many people feel "mixing races" is morally wrong.

Dennis and Diane are proud of their multiracial family. When they adopted Marie and Theresa in May 1975, Diane sent out birth announcements shortly after the girls came home. They read:

> Maybe with God's guidance we will raise human beings who will be leaders of all races. In our home, all races will have lived together in peace, love, and brotherhood.

Dennis is the first to admit that he grew up with feelings of prejudice. But it all changed one day in 1974.

Because of their work with the Vietnamese adoptions, the Nasons were invited to go to Newport on the Oregon coast, where they helped organize a parent-based adoption agency.

The slide show presentation of Kari was one of the highlights in forming the new agency. The Nasons met many people who were adoptive parents. A good number of them already had large families, all had been involved in adoption in some way, and they all shared the same vision. Many of the overseas adoptions had started with the Holt Agency which was based in Creswell, Oregon, and had airlifted hundreds of Korean War orphans to the United States in the 1950's.

By then the Lord had given Diane a vision, and she wasn't about to let go of it. That vision was of children—children everywhere in need. She knew in her heart that she was to help find these children homes and that He would choose the children that He would "bring home."

That vision has continued to be a real conviction with Diane—one that has grown over the years, one she has never lost.

At Newport Dennis and Diane met the couple who had invited them there after reading an article about Kari. They were Ken and Norma Lucas, who had ten children. The Lucases had adopted children from Korea, from the States, and from all over. They were one of the first families in Oregon to adopt transracially.

That visit was the start of a new outlook for Dennis. Since he worked most of the time, he hadn't been as involved as Diane with the adoption work, and he had never considered adopting a black child. They really hadn't discussed it. They had been so involved in Vietnam, committed and convinced of the need in that country.

Ken and Norma had two beautiful black daughters. One was small—about five or six, the same age as the Nasons' Katie Sue.

One day during their visit, Dennis was looking out the window and suddenly grew quiet. Diane went over to see what he was looking at.

Outside Katie and Kim were running hand in hand all around the trees. There was Katie, the blonde, blue-eyed, little girl, and the Lucas's Kim, who was very black with short, close-cropped hair. The contrast was beautiful. They'd become fast friends without a care in the world.

"I've been blind," Dennis said. "I see now that there is no color line with children. The prejudices are all in the adult's mind. I've really changed my thinking."

That comment had special meaning to Diane, because it started Dennis on a new train of thought that brought them closer together—closer to the same vision.

That fall the Nasons led preadopt and postadopt classes. They were involved in the adoption of special needs children and older children in the States. To some it didn't seem as urgent as the needs of Vietnamese orphans, but many children have critical needs.

Norma Lucas gave Diane the names and addresses of contact people to receive adoption books, books supplied by several different states listing children for adoption. These children all had special needs ranging from light to severe handicaps. Special needs may also be due to race or age.

New York had the biggest group for adoption. For every child pictured in the adoption book, there were at least ten others who could take his or her place.

The adoption books were updated every two weeks. The Nasons showed the books to other prospective adoptive parents and explained the different handicaps, medical terms, and disabilities.

While looking at the books, Diane kept returning to a picture of two girls, Marie and Theresa.

The Nasons don't "pick" their children. They feel strongly that God chooses each of their children and "brings them home."

One night Diane was showing a book at a meeting. Dennis was working late and couldn't attend. The Lord seemed to speak to Diane about Theresa and Marie. *These are your children. Bring them home.*

Lord, Diane began to say, *You know we are deep into adoptions here, and Kecia is just getting healthy. Now isn't the time. . . .*

But the message was loud and clear. These were to be their girls.

A few days later while Dennis was attending a meeting of adoptive parents, he paused at a picture of the two girls in the New York adoption book. "Diane," he said, pointing at the pictures, "we've got to talk about these two girls later."

It was Marie and Theresa.

Okay, Lord, Diane thought. *You don't have to hit us both on the head. We're not that dense.*

Both girls had been listed in the books for three years. Marie had a few emotional problems, but both were in perfect physical health. The reasons they hadn't been adopted were twofold: their age, Theresa being ten, Marie eleven, and their black/white parentage.

Dennis and Diane knew the Lord wanted them to have the two girls. They also knew a home study would be difficult because the state had already said "no more." No one can handle more than eight, according to the state, so there's no way they would approve anymore adoptions.

"Lord," Dennis and Diane both prayed, "if you want us to have these girls, you'll have to work it out."

He led the Nasons back to Norma Lucas.

Norma and Ken had often worked through Catholic Services. They weren't Catholic, nor were the Nasons, but it was one of the few adoption agencies operating in southern Oregon.

It is difficult for Dennis and Diane to explain why they do what they do. Most people can't understand it, unless they accept that the Lord commits believers to a certain path and certain way of life that they have no alternative but to follow. The Nasons believe God directs them down that path, just as they, in turn, rely on God one day at a time. It is an important element in their walk with Him.

Norma Lucas called and spoke to Fay Bentley at Catholic Services. "I sort of paved the way," Norma said. Fay agreed to set up an appointment.

She began her meeting with the Nasons by saying, "You both know that I don't advocate large families."

Oh, boy, Diane thought. *A strike against us before we start.*

"However, because of your ability and record of working with children, I've decided to interview you. My decision is not final," Fay went on. "Our board meets in Portland, and they have the final word, but they usually go on my recommendation."

Dennis and Diane were interviewed separately. They also had to have physicals, and then Fay came to the house and talked with the children. The whole process took two months.

In the meantime, three hundred dollars was needed for the cost of the home study. The Nasons were confident that the Lord would provide the money if the girls were supposed to be theirs.

Fay came back for a final visit. She sat down with Dennis and Diane while the children were busy playing elsewhere.

"I've never met a family like yours," she began. "I'm impressed with your family life and how you cope with all the medical hardships; I've no doubt that you could handle two older biracial girls; however, I'm going to recommend against this adoption."

Dennis and Diane were stunned. "But why? We don't understand."

"Because, as I said before, I don't advocate adoptions in families with more than eight children."

Diane feared they were back to Point A, but she had to take a stand against this decision.

"Well, I'm sorry, but you're wrong because we *can* handle whatever God tells us we can handle. When He tells us to quit, then we'll quit. He has us on a pattern and on a road that we don't really control. We know what He wants us to do, and we know who our children are and who we are to bring home. I believe He's pointing us in the right direction with these girls."

"Well, as I told you in the beginning, you can appeal my decision."

Having no other choice, the Nasons asked the board to review the whole home study.

Fay wrote a wonderful report. At the bottom, she gave her main reason for being against the adoption. "This couple already has eight children."

Days passed, a week, then two. No word. Finally, the board representative called.

"We met and reviewed your situation two or three times. We talked with Fay and we believe this is the first time we have done this, but we feel you should have these children over the social worker's objection. We don't believe that objecton is valid in this case."

"Oh, thank you, Lord," Diane cried. "You knew all along, but You certainly gave us some anxious moments."

On May 19, 1975, Marie and Theresa "came home." Theresa was two days past her tenth birthday, and Marie was eleven years old.

Theresa adjusted immediately and became an active part of the family. She was a joy, but she encountered some prejudices at school. One day she came home irate. She pulled her tiny body into a rigid position and said, "Oh, I was so mad today. Do you know what some boy at school called me? He called me a *nigger.*"

"Does that bother you, Theresa?" Diane asked. "It really shouldn't."

She hesitated for a moment. "Well, no, it doesn't, I guess, but coming from that *Mexican,* that's what makes me mad!"

That was typical of Theresa's temper. She could go into a real rage and tell people exactly what she thought. It was a characteristic that would prove to be a real asset to her later on.

A teacher in sixth grade said, "You know, Theresa will be a great achiever. She is just an average student, but she'll always do above average work because of her faith in herself and her belief that she can do it."

Theresa took an interest in 4-H activities and raised calves and a pig and learned to crochet and embroider. She also liked helping Diane prepare for preadopt meetings. Theresa remembered how she felt and how she really wanted to be adopted. It became important for her to help other children find homes. But most of all she became a Christian and a great advocate for the Lord.

Marie balked from the beginning. She wanted to return to her foster parents and later presented a real problem. Dennis and Diane were aware that Marie had emotional problems but were confident that their love and guidance could conquer the rejection she had felt in the past.

Because she was older, she was considered unadoptable by many. The foster parents hadn't told the girls about their true biracial background. Marie thought she was Italian and Jewish, and Theresa believed she was Puerto Rican.

"We always advocate that a child should know and be proud of his or her heritage," Diane said.

What about the current trend of adopted children searching for their biological parents?

"I don't think it's a good idea, unless information is needed to treat a medical problem," Diane said. "Many birth mothers do not want to be found. They have their own families and want to forget the past. If a child discovers this feeling, it can open the wound to further hurt. However, certain bits of information should be shared with the adopted child. I told Lori that her mother was a singer and loved horses."

The Nasons also learned that Marie and Theresa had never been treated like members of the family. When the foster parents went on vacation, Marie and Theresa didn't go. They had never been out of the city or owned a pet.

Diane also learned that the girls had been told they were being adopted so they could work on a farm.

"I can go back to New York anytime I want," Marie taunted. "All I have to do is call and ask."

"Don't be silly, Marie," Theresa said. "*This* is our home now. We've been adopted."

"But I want to go back," Marie insisted.

One of the first things Marie asked for was a pet, and Diane gave her a rabbit. At first Marie took good care of her rabbit, just as she cleaned her bedroom and hung up her clothes. But gradually Marie changed. She stole, lied, hid things, and didn't care about keeping clean.

"Marie," Diane said, "you must shampoo your hair when you bathe tonight."

"All right," Marie said, but then she'd get out of the bathtub without having washed her hair.

"Marie, you've got to change your clothes," Diane said. "Your shirt is dirty."

Marie responded with a blank look. "Okay," she finally said. Still, she wouldn't change.

Notes came home from school.

Marie is difficult to handle. . . .
Today Marie stole all the pastries out of the teachers' lunches in the lounge. . . .
Marie stole money from the students' purses. . . .
She doesn't complete her work. . . .
She seems to be living in another world. . . .
She doesn't get on the bus to come home. Wanders off.

Marie began hoarding food, not to eat, but just to have— under her mattress, under a loose board in the hall, or stuffed in with her clothes. The smell led Diane and the older girls to the rotting food.

For five years, Diane prayed and tried to bring Marie into the reality of her new home, but Marie only got worse. She'd cry out in the middle of the night, and when Diane went to her, she'd cling to Diane and ask, "Why? Why did God let this happen to me?"

"Oh, Marie," Diane would say. "God doesn't let these things happen. There is another person who is very much alive on earth, and that's Satan. Maybe with some outside help, you'll be able to realize that God loves you and wants you to be close to Him and not do all these things."

Diane discussed Marie's problems with Norma, her good friend in adoptions. "She doesn't respond to any form of punishment. She always says she's sorry and doesn't know why she does what she does. I don't know what to think. I don't dare leave her alone for even a minute. She has to be with me, another adult, or confined to her room."

"There's a psychiatrist in Portland," Norma suggested. "I've heard he's quite good with children. I think you should have Marie tested, and the sooner the better."

"Marie is schizophrenic," the psychiatrist told Diane. "She cannot survive in a normal home situation. I'm afraid she needs institutional care."

There was a long waiting list at every institution, but Diane and Dennis had to do something. Leaving Marie in their home could be damaging to the rest of the children. Diane had also discovered that Theresa covered for Marie, something she'd done back in New York.

A halfway home was found that would take Marie until there was a vacancy at the institution.

Diane packed Marie's things, tucking her album in with her pictures and other mementos she'd received over the past few years. The last thing Diane packed was a rag doll. She had made all the girls one for Christmas, and it was one of Marie's most prized possessions.

It was January when Dennis and Diane drove Marie to her new home. Marie was confused and didn't understand what was happening. She smiled as Diane bent down and kissed her good-bye.

"We love you, Marie," she whispered. *And God please take care of her and help her get well,* Diane said under her breath.

Dennis reached for Diane's hand and they hurried to the car and back home to their children—their family.

Marie had been gone two months when the call came that snowy, wintry evening.

"Mrs. Nason?"

"Yes—"

"Do you have a daughter named Marie?"

"Well, yes, but she isn't living with us now. Why do you ask?"

"There's been a fire . . . Marie was trapped inside. They tried to get her out, but it was too late."

When the firemen found Marie she was under the bed, the rag doll Diane had made clutched tightly against her chest.

"She must have gone back for the doll," the woman said at the home. "She was out once—woke everyone else up—helped them out. I know she was out, but she must have gone back inside for that doll."

"Marie will always live in our lives, our hearts," Diane said. "You can't take a child into your home for any length of time and not care about her and not have something about her be engraved on your heart forever. If only we had gotten her sooner, it might have helped."

Chapter Seven

The Twins from Texas

E ven after the fall of Vietnam and the airlifting of babies ceased, the Nasons continued to promote the adoption of the hard-to-place child.

One day Diane phoned an adoption referral agency in California and heard about Sheila and Sherry, black, six-year-old twins from Texas who were handicapped.

"We don't know much about them," the social worker said, "but we understand they need special education. According to the agency they will definitely need special help in school."

What about us? Diane thought. *Was this where the Lord was leading them?* She spoke to Dennis about the twins.

"You know we'll run into a lot of prejudice with black children within our own family," he said.

They did.

"You can't do that," several people commented. "You certainly don't need any more problems for yourself."

What problems? Diane wondered. They were simply things that needed to be dealt with because of the world we live in.

Again, the Nasons heard the cliché that no one can handle more than "X" number of children. Yet the Lord was putting different beliefs in their hearts, and since they felt they were in communication with Him, they had to move ahead.

It was the Nasons' first experience with adoptions in Texas, a state which had just begun to let families from other states adopt children from Texas.

The Nasons' own organization in Oregon had finally been granted a license to place children after many hard-fought battles, many letters, and many points proved to the state. It was one of the first agencies of this sort granted a license and it had started with a parent support group. It was a big step forward, but with the license came restrictions and many standards to be met.

A new home study was required, and the newly licensed agency agreed to do it, so plans began. In adoptions across state lines, the child is represented by a caseworker from his or her own state, plus the caseworker from the state in which the adoptive parents live.

The caseworker from Texas seemed nice, but Diane felt a vague sense of uneasiness. The agency was eager to place the twins, but no additional information was sent regarding their handicaps.

The Nasons met the twins at the airport on a crisp fall day in October 1975. The girls were beautiful. Following a fifteen-minute drive from the airport, Diane knew something was definitely wrong, and it was something that would require more than just a little special help at school. Sherry wasn't steady on her feet, nor could she talk well. Sheila seemed to manage much better.

It was not mealtime, but the girls acted hungry. So Diane offered them a piece of cake. The mess they made was unbelievable, and their eating at mealtime was no better. The Nason children sat with their mouths open and stared. They had never seen anyone eat like this.

"We knew the girls were mentally slow, and we hadn't

been informed," Diane said. "Our own agency hadn't looked into it. It was one of their first experiences with adoption in that state and they thought they had all the needed information. We thought they had too."

Texas had different standards for classifying children for adoption. In addition, special needs children attended various schools depending on the level of their handicapping condition. They were "labeled" slow to severely retarded, as well as biracial and physically handicapped.

Diane tried to enroll the twins in public school, but their test results were very low. The Nasons counseled with several people, but everyone told them that the girls would probably never be able to attend a public school. They first needed up to five years of *intensive* training, which would make them eleven or twelve before they could start first grade. Even then there was no guarantee they could function in a school situation.

Sheila scored slightly higher than Sherry. If the girls could have been separated, Sheila might have been able to go into a concentrated special education program in the public school. But her ties to Sherry pulled her down.

The Nason children had difficulty understanding the twins' problem.

"This happens sometimes," Diane explained. "Some children are so far down the scale they cannot fit into a family situation. They do better in an institutional setting where they can have the necessary intense therapy."

Diane's earlier, uneasy feeling had now been defined. Yet what could they do? Because she and Dennis had more experience than anyone in the field, they were leading other prospective adoptive parents. Now here were two children who were going to have to go back. There simply weren't any state facilities to cope with their needs.

Diane made the necessary call, and the worker agreed

that the twins should be returned. The two girls had not been clearly represented to the Nasons, but the error had resulted from different sets of adoption standards in Texas and Oregon.

Once again, it was an invaluable experience to the Nasons. Because of their experience with Sherry and Sheila, they were now able to tell other people about the different adoption standards in various states and the need for investigation guidelines within local agencies.

It was a depressing time for both Dennis and Diane. They felt that those against the adoption in the first place were pointing their fingers and saying "I told you so."

The Nasons had always given support to other people and now they needed backing and wanted to hear people say, "Hey, I understand. It's ok. These kids cannot stay in a family situation." But only a few came to their defense.

The girls went back to Texas. Because of the Nasons' experience, the Texas and Oregon agencies began to realize that differences in values were extremely important to adoptive families. They needed to know exactly what to expect in any type of adoption.

Six months later, the Lord showed Diane the meaning of that experience. Besides showing the Nasons that they were not infallible, He showed them that some children do not belong in a family, that some adoptions fail. It was an important thing to share with others. *We are still living in this world, and this world isn't perfect. All of us are vulnerable to the events of the world.*

Diane later heard that Sherry's other medical problem had been diagnosed as leukemia, and it was terminal. She had six months to live.

"It would have been difficult for our kids to just watch that little girl die," Dennis said.

Sheila was eventually taken in by a black lady who

wanted a little girl to take care of. That was what Sheila needed—total commitment on a one-to-one basis.

The Lord used the Nasons as steppingstones and opened the eyes of two agencies to the need for better communication in the process. The Nasons gained a humble attitude about adoptions of this type. "Another step had been added in our stairway of learning," Diane said.

She had also discovered pitfalls connected with some adoption agencies.

> They make it difficult for people who want more than eight children and tend to generalize that parents cannot handle more than eight.
> They discourage out-of-state adoptions.
> They discourage the adoption of handicapped children and do not offer education in that area.
> They advocate foster homes rather than adoption for some children. (Adoption results in less need for foster homes, fewer jobs for caseworkers, and less federal money to reimburse state agencies for foster care.)
> They do not always describe a child's true problem.
> They tend to be caught up in bureaucratic red tape and lose sight of the child's needs.
> They do not give individual consideration to each case, each child, and each family wanting to adopt.
> State agencies do not cooperate with private agencies.

In overseas adoptions there were additional problems: multitudes of forms to be completed for the immigration office, many legal documents, lengthy waits, and additional expense.

In light of all this, the Nasons were encouraged because at least one agency in ten cared about children and wanted to see them in a loving home. And a loving home was just what the Nasons wanted to provide.

Chapter Eight

Donny

After the problems encountered with Sheila and Sherry, Marie, and Bill, the Nasons felt the need to reassess what they were doing and why they were doing it. Their faith hadn't wavered, but they had some doubts about whether they were really doing what God wanted them to do in the lives of children.

In the spring of 1976, they had a beautiful family of ten children, and their home life was super. They kept busy with all the children and their various activities. They continued to help others involved in adoption on an individual basis and maintained the adoption books showing available children, but they let other people they had assisted in adoptions take over some preadopt meetings.

Dennis and Diane felt the need for more inner strength, and decided to conduct Bible studies in their home. They had always held Bible studies within their own family, but now they wanted to study with people who shared their vision. It turned out to be a spiritually uplifting time for all.

One Sunday morning in March, Diane and Dennis were in an adult Sunday school class when a wave of sickness hit Diane. She had been troubled the past few days with lingering flu symptoms. Her energy was at low ebb. Since she was rarely sick and always had enough energy for everything, she wondered what was wrong. She had all the symptoms of being pregnant but felt it was impossible. Lisa, their last biological child, was ten. On a whim, and without telling Dennis, Diane bought a pregnancy kit and made the test.

The Sunday school was discussing the subject of families and how pregnancy can come as a shock when a couple thinks their family is complete.

Diane poked Dennis in the ribs. "You don't know how true that subject is," she said. "Things happen like that, and they happen to everybody."

"Yeah, I know," he said, "but it would never happen to us. It's been ten years since we've had a baby."

"It's happened," Diane said, trying to stifle a smile.

The class ended. Dennis and Diane didn't go to church. They went to their car and talked for an hour.

They were both overwhelmed at the prospect of having another child. It didn't seem possible, yet they realized what it meant. *A new little Nason.* This child was going to be very special. They had experienced a lot of pain and gone through many levels of adjustment. The Lord had chosen this time, while they were sitting back and evaluating, to give them a beautiful normal baby.

It all fits into place, Diane reflected. *Isn't that always the way with God's timing? He knows what He is doing. He has a definite plan, a purpose for everything He allows to happen, but we earthlings doubt and question and complain and wonder.*

In the meantime, Diane heard about a Christian doctor who was supposed to be tops in the field. Diane and Dennis were thrilled over their "miracle baby" and were full of anticipation. The doctor looked at Diane's chart, noting that she'd had problems with past pregnancies, that her age was thirty-three, and that it had been ten years since her last baby was born.

"I suggest," he went on, "due to all this information, that an abortion is your logical choice."

Diane was stunned. Here was a Bible-believing doctor recommending she abort her own baby!

Diane jumped to her feet and lashed out, "I'm sorry, doctor, but I'm in the wrong office!"

Blinded by angry tears, she hurried out of that office and found another doctor, a nice, kind, gentle person. He knew how excited the Nasons were about their baby and thought it was terrific too.

"I don't foresee any problems at all. Don't worry. We'll keep a close eye on you during the pregnancy."

It was the encouragement Diane needed. The pregnancy progressed and she had a lot of support. The children were ecstatic. Kecia, the youngest, was two and a half, hardly a baby anymore.

"We want a girl," the girls said.

"The girls outnumber the boys," Mark, Scott, and Bill chanted. "It's got to be a boy!"

After a bout with two wisdom teeth and the usual morning nausea, Diane enjoyed her pregnancy. Dennis pampered her, bringing her a single rose now and then. Sometimes after the little ones had eaten, they would leave the older kids to babysit and go out for dinner. (It was as if they knew busy days were ahead of them and that within the next eighteen months four children would join the Nason family.)

Dennis and Diane attended natural childbirth classes—something they hadn't done before—and they were enthusiastic. Dennis was especially excited about the possibility of helping with the birth.

When the time approached for delivery, Diane couldn't help feeling apprehensive as she recalled Lisa's difficult birth.

But the Lord was there, and Diane knew it. There were four in that delivery room—Diane, Dennis, the doctor, and God.

When the birth was imminent, the doctor yelled, "Dennis, get down here. This is *your* baby. I want you to deliver it."

"I'll be right there," Dennis said excitedly.

At 3 P.M. on October 8, 1976, Donald Robert Nason made his appearance. "I heard his first cry and then they laid him on my tummy," Diane said. "From that moment, a closeness, love, and bonding started."

After calling home to tell the children, Diane couldn't wait to call her dad, since Donny was his namesake. From the first, Donny was his grandpa's boy.

Since the Fehlmans lived nearby, Grandpa and Donny saw each other every day. From the time Donny could walk, Grandpa would come to the house and would say, "Well, Donny, are you ready to go for your lesson?"

And out they went, hand in hand, to explore. They explored the hay, animals, and flowers. Grandpa shared his knowledge with the dark-haired boy. Since Grandpa was a rock hound, he'd point out a rock and say, "That's an igneous rock, and this is a jasper."

Grandpa loved all the kids, and each Christmas he donned his Santa Claus outfit and arrived at the Nason household to pass out presents. As the children got older, they knew who it was, but it was always great fun for the little ones. Excited and giggling, they would crawl onto Santa's lap and give him a big hug.

With Donny's birth came a rebirth in the Nasons' dedication to adoption and to children who wait to be adopted.

Identical to Mark in looks, Donny was like having Mark

all over again, only this time they had a healthy baby. Dennis and Diane felt it was God's way of giving them the fun and enjoyment of having a child with normal health and development.

Donny was to be a role model. He had been strategically placed by the Lord, because the Lord knew about the three little ones about to arrive who were close to his age: a brother and two sisters handicapped in various degrees. They would need the stimulation and challenge of normal childhood development on their own level to progress and grow.

One of the new little sisters, Mandy, came from India and brought shigella, a disease of high fever and bloody diarrhea. Soon nearly every member in the Nason household had come down with it. Donny, who was eighteen months old, was the first to become sick.

It started with a high fever. Tepid water baths and aspirin were tried, but nothing kept Donny's fever down. Grandma Fehlman came and held him for hours. On the second day the church elders came and prayed over the small boy.

The following afternoon Diane was preparing the evening meal while keeping an eye on Donny, who was lying on the couch. When she went to pick him up before calling the others in to dinner, he suddenly threw his head back and went into a convulsion. Diane had been through a lot of emergencies—trips with Mark to the hospital, rushing Scott in when he needed stitching up—but never had she been so frightened. Donny's eyes rolled back into his head and he quit breathing. He lay there in her arms, his eyes and mouth open.

"Jesus, help me!" Diane cried. She started giving him mouth-to-mouth resuscitation, then yelled for the older girls to put dinner on the table and to watch everyone. "I've got to get Donny to the hospital."

Even as she said it, she wondered *how*, with Dennis gone.

Suddenly Mark pulled into the driveway in his little car. He was just coming home from school.

"I've got to get Donny to the hospital!" Diane cried.

"Rogue Valley?"

She nodded. All the way there, Diane gave Donny mouth-to-mouth. Just as they arrived Donny opened his eyes and looked at his mother. He had started breathing on his own but Diane rushed him into the emergency room anyway.

The doctor on duty ran several tests and found nothing.

"Could it be shigella?" Diane asked. "We adopted this little girl from India and she was sick with it on her way here, but was fine when she arrived."

The doctor shrugged. "Well, maybe, but we've never had that here. It's not really the symptoms I see, but I'll run some blood tests."

Diane was still shaking. "Oh, Mark, that was so close."

"I know," he said. "Sure reminds me of some times when we were together in the hospital."

Diane smiled. "Yes, it sure does."

The doctor finally tracked the problem down—it was shigella.

Donny was put into isolation and Diane stayed with him for two days. Then she came down with the disease.

Shigella takes a long time to get over, and soon other family members were admitted. Donny was weak for a month afterwards but soon gained back the weight he had lost.

Grandpa was glad to have his walking buddy back, and the hikes resumed. Even after the Nasons moved to Sisters in 1979, Grandpa and Grandma Fehlman came to visit once a month. They were precious times, but nobody realized then how precious.

The closeness Donny and his grandpa felt was brought to a crushing, sudden end in February 1980 when a speeding

Diane and her Dad riding at the ranch, 1952.

The Nason family begins,
June 26, 1960.

Don Fehlman, Diane's dad, captured in a favorite pose by grandson Mark.

Dr. William J. Miller, Christian friend and physician to the Nasons.

Grandma Fehlman helped Katie celebrate her twelfth birthday.

Mandy. A lady can always manage to comb her hair. *(Gail Denham Photo)*

Billy Joe has found a special encourager in older sister Lori *(Gail Denham Photo)*.

Donny and Kecia 'ride herd' on Scott's dairy cattle. *(Gail Denham Photo)*

Lisa Lyn

Theresa Michelle

Lori Diane

Kari Marie

Katie Sue

Dorell Dawn

Nancie Carol

Photos of Lisa, Theresa, Lori, and Kari by *T. J. Smallwood Photography.*
Photos of Katie, Dorell, Nancie and Kecia by *Beattie Stabeck, National School Studios, Inc.*

Mandy Ann Teresa

Melissa Jean

Kecia Ruth

Diana Louise

Cynthia Janet

Marie Louise
(deceased)

Mark Andrew
(Ake Lundberg Photo)

Dennis Scott

Gary Daymon
(Ake Lundberg Photo)

Bill
(Lithia Park Studio)

Jeffrey Richard
(Ake Lundberg Photo)

Darin Daniel
*(T. J. Smallwood
Photography)*

Daniel Joshua
*(Beattie Stabeck,
National School
Studios, Inc.)*

Daryl John
*(Beattie Stabeck,
National School
Studios, Inc.)*

Robert Harold

Donald Robert
*(Beattie Stabeck,
National School
Studios, Inc.)*

David Lee
*(Beattie Stabeck,
National School
Studios, Inc.)*

Kevin Martin

Kenneth Christian

Richard Patterson
(Ake Lundberg Photo)

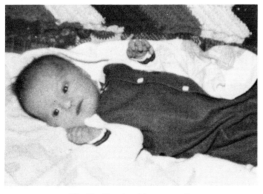

Martin Paul   (deceased)

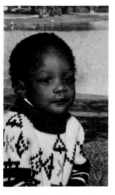

William Joseph

A moment of fun and relaxation for Dennis and Diane.

Mark and Terri with Nicole, the first Nason grandchild.

Home for the Celebration Family in Sisters, Oregon —before the latest addition. *(Gail Denham Photo)*

truck hit the Fehlmans' Datsun pickup as Grandpa was turning into his own driveway.

The whole family was numb, and it was twelve days of agonizing confusion for the small three-and-a-half-year-old Donny. Why did Grandpa have to be hurt and go to the hospital? He didn't understand, when he was in Grandpa's house, why Grandpa wasn't there to take him for a walk.

"I'll wait here until he comes out," Donny said, confident that Grandpa would come home soon from the hospital.

Dennis and Diane and the younger ones stayed at the Fehlman home with Diane's mother for five days. When Don's condition did not improve, they went home, tended to things there, then turned around and drove back to Ashland.

Diane's brother Jerry and his wife Geraldine came from Idaho. On the final day they all came home from the hospital at 9 P.M. At eleven o'clock, they were summoned back.

Diane and Geraldine stayed behind with the little ones while Dennis, Jerry, Mark, and Lyn Fehlman hurried to the hospital.

"My dad is dying," Diane said. "I know this is it."

At 11:30, Donny bolted upright in his bed and started screaming. Sweat was pouring from him. Diane rushed to him, holding him close. "Honey, what's *wrong*?"

"Grandpa's gone," he cried. "My grandpa died. He won't be with me anymore."

A few minutes later, the phone rang. It was Dennis: "He's gone, Diane. It's over."

"What time?" Diane asked.

"Eleven-thirty," Dennis said. "We just got there, and right after that he passed on. He's with the Lord now."

Diane told him about Donny's waking and crying, and Dennis was amazed. Later, as Diane analyzed it, she realized it wasn't that amazing. Grandpa and grandson were so close, and Diane believes that the spirits of some people are so intertwined that they feel things deeply together and about each other. They had been like one.

Dennis and Diane took all the children to the funeral. Dennis held Donny as the minister gave a short memorial, mentioning how much Don had loved the children and the effect his life had on their upbringing. It was difficult for Diane to realize that her father was gone. It wasn't as hard to accept his death as it was to accept the unnecessary way it had happened.

Donny continued to grieve. Many times he would cry in his play, then go to Diane and say how much he missed Grandpa. They tried to comfort him, but it was something Donny had to get over in his own way. He talked to his grandma on the telephone, and that helped to reassure him that Grandma was still there and cared.

Six months after Grandpa's death, another strange thing happened. Donny woke screaming in his bed.

Dennis ran to him. The small child was sweaty and shaking all over. "Grandpa was just here and now he's gone," Donny cried.

Dennis tried to calm him down, but Donny insisted. "No. He was here. I saw him and he told me that he couldn't come right now, that he couldn't be with me, but that he'd always watch out for me. But Daddy, I wish he could come."

"I wish so too," Dennis said.

The next morning Mark called from Ashland.

"You're not going to believe this," he began, "but last night I had a dream. I'm not even sure it was a dream. It was about Grandpa. He talked to me. I woke up sobbing and he told me he was awaiting judgment and that he was fine and he would always be watching out for me."

Diane could hardly believe it. She believed in guardian

angels and she knew that both boys had been close to their grandfather—so close that maybe he wasn't quite ready to leave them. She feels that her father is their very special guardian angel. Her faith has been reaffirmed that God can do beautiful things, even through tragedy.

Another incident happened when Donny was five. Diane was reading a preschool readiness book to him when the phone rang. It was Dennis calling from work. Suddenly Donny began crying as he looked out the window.

"What's wrong?" Diane cried, asking Dennis to hold on a minute.

"Grandpa came again," Donny said. "Just now, up there in the sky." He pointed. "I saw him next to Jesus. I want him to come so bad, but I know he can't. I just know he's there."

Dennis talked to Donny on the phone and calmed him.

"I sure miss him," Donny said.

The next day Mark called from work to find out how everyone was.

"I've been having some strange experiences," he said. "Yesterday during the day, I was walking downtown and when I turned around, Grandpa was right behind me. I looked again and he was gone. It was just like he was following me to make sure I was all right."

Diane loaned Mark her copy of Billy Graham's book, *Angels: God's Secret Agents*, hoping it would help him understand a little more.

Grandpa's presence hasn't been felt since. Diane interprets it as a final reassurance and farewell to the boys.

One more incident reveals the closeness and concern Don Fehlman felt for his daughter's family.

Lyn called one day about a month after her husband's death. She was crying on the phone.

"Diane," she said, "I've been out in the shop with all of

your dad's rock equipment, trying to sort out some drawers. I came across this manila envelope that said, 'Unpaid medical bills.' It was a letter in Daddy's handwriting and addressed to Donny. It said, 'For Donny. Put it in the bank and get principal and interest on his eighteenth birthday, for college. If he doesn't go to college, it's to be divided between Mark, Scotty, Lisa, Diana, and Donny. Grandpa, with all my love.'"

The manila envelope contained many one- and five-dollar bills amounting to $1,200. Diane couldn't believe it. Her father had saved the money in a year's time from his Social Security payments and retirement. He had sold a few rock items on the side, but mainly it was just saved from his income. Lyn had wondered why he never seemed to have money when she asked him to go to the store, and now she knew why.

Diane feels that her father knew his time was short and that he wanted to leave something special for his little grandson.

Since that time, Grandma Fehlman has moved to the Sisters area, and Donny has a grandparent close by again.

This biological child, named for Diane's father, brought special love and a renewed sense of God's will to many people.

Chapter Nine

Danny

Diane went to her mailbox on February 25, 1977, and found a letter from Lya Engelken, a special friend working with her own adoption agency in Georgia. Diane and Lya had become friends during their involvement in Vietnamese adoptions and had continued their friendship by mail.

"Diane," the letter began. "I have a four-year-old handicapped boy in El Salvador who desperately needs a home. He has severe malnutrition, curvature of the spine, and a limp from a hip defect. Would you be interested?"

Diane called Dennis at work.

"I imagine the cost is tremendous," Dennis said.

"You're right," Diane agreed. "Twenty-five hundred dollars is inconceivable, but it can happen through Him—one step at a time."

"Yes, nothing is impossible with the Lord. Let's pray about it."

Three days later, the answer was confirmed and Diane called Lya. "He's a Nason, Lya. We'll bring him home."

"Great!" Lya said. "I'll call El Salvador today and get back to you as soon as I hear something."

The obstacles were many, but one by one they were overcome. Daniel Joshua (named because of the many battles he had to overcome) was about to have a new home and family.

State requirements had to be met again for this overseas adoption. An update of the most recent home study would be started upon receipt of $230. Money was a big obstacle. Living one day at a time on faith, one learns to expect miracles, but this would take a *big* miracle.

"Diane, you'll need to send $380 by Monday to start the legal paperwork," Lya said when she called.

"Wow!" Diane said. "That makes $610 due in three days. It's up to the Lord now."

Friday's mail came. Only five weeks after filing their return, the Nasons' tax refund arrived. Diane was excited. "Dennis," she cried, "after paying our farm loan we're only short $80."

"It may as well be $800," Dennis said. "You know payday is two weeks away."

"Maybe a miracle will happen on Monday," Diane said.

Monday came and as Diane hurried to the mailbox, she thought, *This is Danny's day, surely there'll be something!*

There was. A check for $82 from the San Francisco office of Internal Revenue—a refund from farm production. Diane had no idea it was coming. They had never received it before, nor have they received it since, but there it was—a real miracle.

Dennis nearly dropped the receiver when Diane called to tell him. "It's the total amount we need. Who says the Lord can't provide everything!"

Their faith was totally strengthened. But there were more obstacles to overcome.

"Sure, Diane, you know I'll help," Senator Lenn Hannon from southern Oregon said. "That little guy needs to come to a loving home and soon. I'll give you the addresses of some other senators and congressmen who can help."

The obstacle they faced now was the limitation of only two visas per family for overseas adoptions, and the Nasons had used the two for their Vietnamese daughters. Legislation was needed to acquire a visa for Danny.

Diane wrote Senator Mark Hatfield concerning the visa limitation, and mentioned the urgency of bringing Danny home. On March 10, Senator Hatfield replied with a letter indicating his willingness to help.

On April 14, Diane received confirmation of Senator Hatfield's intent to submit a private bill before Congress on Danny's behalf. He asked for cosponsors, more telephone calls, and more letters.

On April 20, Oregon Congressman Jim Weaver agreed to sponsor the bill in the House. On April 25, Oregon Senator Bob Packwood sent the Nasons a letter saying he would be happy to cosponsor the bill with Senator Hatfield.

Time passed. Dennis and Diane prayed, as did others.

Riki Poster, Senator Hatfield's aide, was in touch constantly.

Telephone calls crisscrossed the country (and beyond) nearly every day—to Portland; McMinnville; Georgia; Washington, D.C.; and to El Salvador—and back again. The phone bill totalled $300. Riki kept checking with the immigration service officials in Washington.

There has to be another way, Diane felt. While waiting for the legislation to pass, there had to be a way to move without depending on that bill to go through all the channels.

Immigration officials said there was another way, but it would have to originate in El Salvador. A medical visa could be issued at the discretion of El Salvador officials, but they required many documents.

Dennis and Diane gathered all the official papers from birth certificates to financial responsibility to medical care available in the United States. The information was on its way in two days, then came more waiting and phoning.

Finally, there was an answer from El Salvador: Request denied on the grounds that Danny could survive in El Salvador. It wasn't a matter of life or death.

Diane and Dennis were discouraged, yet they knew the Lord was working everything out.

Riki tried again at the Immigration Service. They had decided there was another way, strictly through Immigration and the United States State Department. It was called an Advance Parole. It would permit Danny to enter the United States on the basis of medical and humanitarian reasons. The passage of the private bill would make Danny's status permanent, but in the meantime he could be home receiving all the loving care he needed while awaiting passage of the bill.

More documents were needed, as well as pictures of Danny and calls to Immigration officials in Portland. After two days the needed prayers and papers were on their way to Portland.

Danny's case was reviewed and passed at the state level and sent to Washington for final Immigration Service approval.

Diane called Riki and Lya, and they rejoiced together. Maybe this was the way at last.

One week later an official letter arrived: "Request denied"—not for medical or humanitarian reasons, but because the Nasons had already used two visas, and this action might set a precedent.

All the documents were returned, and the Nasons were back to the start of the visa problem.

Again, Dennis and Diane were deeply disappointed. "I know Danny is coming," Diane said. "The Lord will bring him home somehow."

Diane called Riki and told her about the denial. She was taken aback. "I just knew it would work out this time." She hesitated for a moment. "Listen, give me a few days. Then I'll get back to you, okay?"

After Senator Hatfield heard about it, he personally contacted the new director of Immigration who had just come into office. It was ironic that the new director of Immigration Service for the United States was Hispanic.

Three days later on the last day of school, when Diane had been enjoying a fun day with all the children, a call came from Washington. Riki was on the line.

"Diane, you'd better sit down," Riki said. "I've been trying to reach you all day."

Diane's heart nearly stopped. The decision had been reversed by the new Immigration director. Danny could enter the United States on Advance Parole visa. El Salvador would be notified immediately.

"Praise the Lord," was all Diane could say. "Praise Him for working through so many dedicated people."

In the meantime, after the first refusal by Immigration, Lya had been in contact with the Nasons. Her representative in El Salvador had discovered that, miracle of miracles, the two-and-a-half-year wait for a non-preference visa had been moved up to June 1, making them eligible to apply for a non-preference visa for Danny. Many official documents were needed immediately in El Salvador. They were sent by June 1, because the status would only be current in June.

Now the only remaining obstacle involved the balance of the money. There were the Friends of Children adoption fee, travel expenses in flying to El Salvador, staying three days, then bringing Danny home. The minimum required would be an additional $1,200. It was another big hurdle, but Dennis and Diane and several others prayed. They were confident that somehow the Lord would overcome the final problem.

Throughout 1976 and early 1977, the Nasons had been negotiating with a neighbor to buy the property adjoining theirs to complete the farm. They needed some additional acres just to produce more hay as feed for more cows to butcher for their freezer.

The neighbor wouldn't negotiate on the Nasons' terms at all. They decided the land must not be meant to be theirs after all.

On May 1, the neighbor called and agreed to sell on their terms. Dennis and Diane were excited and proceeded to refinance the farm, to include the price agreed on.

The contract was drawn up on June 1, the exact date of confirmation of Danny's homecoming. The only difference was that the owner of the property they were purchasing had dropped the price by $1,200 because he felt repairs were needed on the property. The contract, already written up and going through the loan office, had been approved. The money was on its way. That provided them with the $1,200 cash needed for Danny's trip home.

"The Lord told us this was our child," Diane said. "He did everything He could possibly do to bring little Daniel Joshua Nason home."

On Friday, June 17, Diane called Lya to find out if there had been a final date set and if Danny's trip home could be arranged.

No word from El Salvador.

They called the American Consulate in El Salvador. After twenty minutes the file was located. The communication was complete. Only the day before a cable had been received and the Advance Parole approval had arrived. A letter would be typed that day giving Danny entry into the United States.

The court procedure would be only one day in this case.

(It usually took three to four days.) "No more documents needed. Come to get your son."

They were beautiful words. The miracle had unfolded in four months. The Lord had moved two governments, provided $2,500, and touched the hearts of countless people—all because of one little boy.

Diane called and told every person connected with Danny, "He's coming home. We're making travel arrangements now."

Chapter Ten

A Miracle in El Salvador

When the endless paperwork was finally completed for adopting Danny, the Nasons decided Dennis was the logical one to go to El Salvador for the boy since Diane was needed by the children at home.

On Monday, June 21, Dennis was scheduled to leave Medford at 10 A.M. for a flight to Portland where he would meet with immigration officials to complete investigations on the private bill. Then he would go on to Los Angeles and from there to Miami. He would arrive in Miami at 6 A.M. Tuesday and pick up Danny's original documents, which had been flown to Miami from Georgia. Dennis would be on his way to El Salvador by 7 A.M.

Diane had arranged Dennis's itinerary down to the smallest detail, but he was still worried about making the appointment at the courthouse with the immigration official in Portland. After the plane landed, assuming it was on time, he had less than thirty minutes to make it to the courthouse, and he didn't know where it was.

As the Lord often does, He placed the right person in Dennis's path that morning. Dan O'Dell, an old friend in adoptions who was on the same flight into Portland, just happened to have a rented car waiting and was headed downtown. Of course he could drop Dennis off at the courthouse—no problem.

When Dennis arrived—ten minutes ahead of time—he was nervous. He was a spokesman for the Nason family and wanted to make a good impression. This official would hear the story of why Dennis was going to El Salvador, and would have the final say that would okay the trip.

"Did you bring all the paperwork?" the official asked.

"I sure did," Dennis answered.

He began leafing through the papers. "How many kids do you have? Tell me about them."

Dennis began talking, starting at the beginning. "Our oldest son, Mark, was a severe asthmatic."

"My boy was a severe asthmatic, too."

"If it hadn't been for the post office, we wouldn't have been able to afford the insurance," Dennis went on.

The official chuckled. "You know, I started out as a postal clerk before I switched over to immigration."

Dennis sensed the ice was broken and began to relax.

Next the official got out the big packet of folders which Diane had carefully put together.

"Of course, you know the birth dates of each one of your children, and you know the day the adoptions were finalized?"

Dennis's heart sank. "You gotta be kidding. Will you run that by me one more time, slowly?"

The official nodded. "I figured you wouldn't have that information. You'll have to call your wife."

"From here?"

"Sure, there's a phone. No problem. It's just part of our job to check these things out."

Diane didn't answer the phone. Then Dennis remembered she had planned to take the dog to the veterinarian.

Come on, Diane, hurry home, Dennis thought as the minutes ticked away.

He called again, and she was there. "I need the birth dates and adoption degrees of every one of the kids."

"Run that by me one more time, slowly," she said. Then they started laughing.

"I'll look them up and call you right back," Diane replied.

Ten minutes later Diane had located everything and was able to rattle off the figures.

"There's one final step," the immigration official said. "You need to be fingerprinted."

He wished Dennis luck and said the only thing left was to check with the American Embassy in El Salvador.

When Dennis arrived in Los Angeles, he went to four different terminals before he found the right flight to Miami. "When you go from a little town like Ashland, Oregon, to a big city like Los Angeles, it's instant lost," Dennis said to one of the airport attendants.

The old doubts came back as Dennis boarded the plane and looked at his itinerary again. What if Danny's papers weren't in Miami? He also remembered horror stories he had heard about Montezuma's revenge. One family went down to pick up a child, became desperately ill, and ended up in the hospital. Dennis decided he might try fasting the whole time he was in El Salvador.

The plane to Miami ran into head winds and arrived twenty minutes late. He would really have to hustle to pick up the papers and make his flight. Then came an announcement on the intercom:

"Would Mr. Nason please pick up some papers after landing?"

The documents had arrived. "Praise the Lord!" Dennis said aloud.

"I'm looking for some papers—I'm Mr. Nason," Dennis

said to the first attendant he saw once he was off the plane.

"They're at the United Airlines counter."

"I've only got ten minutes to catch the Spanish Central American flight." He glanced around. The terminal was huge.

"You can make it," was the answer. "Your flight is not far away."

"We don't have your papers, Mr. Nason," a crisp voice said. "They're at Northwest Orient."

With only five minutes to go, Dennis hurried down to Northwest.

"Oh, no, we sent them over to Pacific."

Hey, Lord, what's going on here? Dennis wondered. Here he was, all 230 pounds, racing like mad, carrying his bag, dripping sweat, and feeling like he was dying. He wasn't used to the humidity in Miami. A sudden chill hit him. He wasn't going to get those papers. He was going to miss his flight. Another chill hit. *Hey, Lord, why is this happening?*

It was now two minutes until the flight departure.

I don't know how I'm going to do it, but I'll have to go to El Salvador without the papers and pray for the best.

Just as Dennis approached the Pacific counter, the flight attendant said, "You must be Mr. Nason. We're waiting for you. Oh, yes, we have some papers for you." She handed him a folder.

"Thank God," Dennis said, clutching the papers as he hurried onto the plane.

Totally exhausted, Dennis found a seat and sank back. He couldn't believe it. He was a sweating, nervous wreck, and he hadn't even left the country yet.

The stewardess began instructing passengers in Spanish to fasten their seat belts, and Dennis realized he was the only one who looked American, and probably the only one who spoke English.

From his seat, he could look into the cockpit, and he

noticed the pilot staring at him. The pilot whispered something to the stewardess, who then came back to Dennis and repeated the whole routine in English.

A few minutes later breakfast was served. Dennis did a double take when he discovered an enchilada smothered in chili sauce. He tried it but couldn't finish.

The stewardess looked offended. "You don't like our food?"

"Oh, yes, it's good. I'm just awfully nervous."

"I can see that," she answered. "You're sweating all over."

There was a forty-five-minute layover in Nicaragua, and Dennis decided to go into the terminal to look around. The pilot called him aside as he was leaving the plane.

"Why are you going to El Salvador?" he asked.

Dennis told him about Danny and the rest of the kids at home and how all the Nasons were eager to have Danny join their family.

"I wish you a lot of luck," the pilot said.

Dennis got off the plane and walked into the terminal. He bought a coffee mug for Diane just as the loudspeaker announced it was time to reboard the plane.

Dennis had noticed armed guards along the runway and around the airfield. As he joined the line of passengers, two men with machine guns began checking everyone before they reboarded. Dennis wasn't worried until he heard the armed men ask the man directly in front of him for his boarding pass. Then they looked at Dennis and said, "Pass?"

He didn't have a pass. He had been the last one off the plane, and apparently the stewardess had failed to give him one. *Lord, what's happening now?* he wondered. There he was, old Doubting Dennis again, but this time he had a machine gun pointed at his belly.

"No pass, no plane," said the men and took Dennis to a

corner. Stories about innocent people being locked up in jail went through Dennis's mind as he heard the plane's motor revving up.

Lord, they're going to leave without me. You can't let them do this. What's going on here? Dennis felt like he was having a heart attack right on the spot.

The stewardess came off the plane and talked to the guards. "No," they told her. There was no way they were going to let Dennis back on the plane.

I'm going to be locked up, he thought. *I'll be down here the rest of my life. This can't be happening.*

A few minutes later, the pilot walked off the plane. Dennis didn't catch what the pilot said or did; but he gave the guards something, and they let Dennis get back on the plane. If the pilot hadn't looked back and noticed that Dennis's seat was empty, he would have left without the nervous American.

Dennis sat motionless in his seat. He felt dead. He had died two hours ago. He knew he wasn't going to make it to El Salvador. He would never see Danny, never see Diane or the kids again.

But the plane landed, and the first thing Dennis noticed was the beautiful country with its lush, green grass, tall trees, and beautiful shrubs. Again, there were guards at the fence and for a moment Dennis panicked.

He had been told what to say to the taxi driver and how to get to the apartment where he would be staying. He got his papers and short-time visa, exchanged some money, then looked for a taxi. He waved at one, then another, but no one picked him up.

Suddenly a trooper approached. "Say, can't you get a cab?" he asked.

"No, and I don't speak Spanish," Dennis answered.

"I can help you. I'll tell the driver where you want to go."

Nobody explained to Dennis that there was only one flight into El Salvador each day, and that if a taxi driver drives to San Salvador quickly enough, he can head back to the airport and make a second trip. More trips, more money.

"No problem," the taxi driver said. "I know right where you are going."

The driver headed down the country road. He drove a 1950 car and traveled sixty miles per hour; Dennis was sure it would fall apart.

Lord, he prayed, *help a bus, car, or anything to get in front of this taxi, because he isn't going to slow down otherwise.*

The driver talked all the time, while Dennis held onto the seat. Two near accidents and two near heart attacks later, he was still clutching the side of the seat, his face pale. *Lord*, he continued to pray, *if I ever get home again, I'll be only too happy.*

Finally he dared to look out the window. As far as he could see were rows of huts, each with a tin roof, a big open door and two windows. There were people sitting in the dirt in the huts that reminded Dennis of the pig barns at home. It was hard to believe that people lived like that.

They finally arrived in San Salvador. The driver raced through town, narrowly missing people as he drove up over curbs and back down. Dennis prayed for his own safety, and for those innocent people on the sidewalks.

They came to the little apartment on Marko Street where he would be staying and was scheduled to meet Judy Quintana. She would take Dennis to the judge who had done all the paperwork. Dennis met his host, who spoke English and assured Dennis that the water was okay to drink. Dennis decided to go on to the embassy first and take care of his business there before meeting Judy at ten o'clock.

"I'll take you to the embassy," his host said.

"It's just two blocks," Dennis said. "I'll make it."

"No." The voice was firm. "You have to learn how to walk down here. You just don't step out onto the street."

"I'm sure I can manage."

But the man insisted, and later Dennis was glad. On the short two-block walk, they were nearly run down by motorists three times.

There was more hassle at the embassy. "We never had advance paroles before," the consul said. "We don't think this is right. He—the boy you are adopting—should have to wait for a number."

"What's the real problem here?" Dennis asked. "Aren't we here for one thing—to give love and a family to a child? The visa has already been granted. There's no use in getting upset with each other."

Forty-five minutes later, the man, who turned out to be from Oregon, was satisfied. "Okay, we'll bury the ax and get down to it." He approved everything and said, "You may have a problem tomorrow going back to the airport, because the airlines are fined heavily if they find they are taking back an illegal alien. Since this is a first, they may not accept this paper. Then you call me and I'll come get it straightened out. In that case, we'll have to make new arrangements for your flight back."

This can't happen, Dennis thought. *I don't have enough money to stay longer. I wasn't prepared for this kind of emergency.*

Things were quiet when Dennis returned to the street, but people were acting scared. Suddenly he heard machine-gun fire and everyone hit the ground—everyone except Dennis. He ran the two blocks back to the apartment, his feet barely touching the pavement. Bullets flew everywhere as he pounded on the door.

Minutes later, things quieted down. Judy arrived, and Dennis asked her about the shooting.

"Oh, you were at the embassy when that went on?"

"I'd just walked out the door."

"Communist guerillas came in and shot down four policemen right on the street."

"I heard shells ricocheting but didn't wait to find out what was going on."

"It's a good thing," she said. "Let's go see Danny now. We'll go to the judge, and you let me do the talking first, okay?"

They got into her Volkswagen bus, and Dennis noticed a guard on every corner.

"It's all politics," Judy said. "It's really gotten bad the last few days. You just never know in this country."

They arrived at the judge's chambers, and Dennis saw his son for the first time. He wasn't prepared for the small child with a shaven head. He looked so different from his picture. Dennis choked up and tears came to his eyes.

"Hey, you're not supposed to show any emotion, okay? You're supposed to be big and brave," Judy said.

"Oh yeah, right." He sat down to fill out the paperwork, but all he wanted to do was hold Danny.

The judge had to approve the family, and Dennis had to show that he could help with the child's medical problem—the main reason for the approval of the Advance Parole.

Then it was Dennis's turn to talk; Judy would interpret. The judge began arguing vehemently with Judy. *Oh, no,* Dennis thought. *He doesn't like me. Or our family. The adoption is off.*

But the judge was simply trying to understand why, with all the kids in El Salvador, Dennis would choose one that was crippled and wouldn't be able to do much.

"We want to help him," Dennis responded. "We knew he was crippled, and that's why we chose him."

"All right," the judge said. "The only stipulation is that you must send a picture every three months and keep in touch."

They got the passport. Dennis took Danny into his arms and hugged him tight, then Judy drove them back to the apartment.

Danny was frightened and wouldn't let Dennis out of his sight. The only words he knew were "Mama" and "Poppa." He seemed hungry, so Dennis gave him a glass of milk, which he gulped down. But it was too rich for his digestive system, since he was used to only one meal a day, usually rice and a tortilla. Later he sat on the toilet for two hours.

"I guess we'd better eat a light lunch," Dennis said.

Dennis had been told to wash Danny's head with special soap to get rid of any lice and decided it would be easier just to get into the shower with him and scrub him down. The miracle came as the two walked out of the shower. This little boy with curvature of the spine, a twisted leg, and a slight hump—was healed! Almighty God healed him right there on the spot!

Danny had to be handicapped to go before the judge. He had to have a physical defect to qualify for the advance parole to get out of El Salvador. With that hurdle passed, God had now healed him completely. God was still in control, taking care of every minute detail.

When they went down to lunch, the people in the building were amazed that Danny was walking straight.

"He was healed," Dennis told them.

They just looked at him and smiled.

That afternoon Dennis and Danny walked over to the embassy so Dennis could take a picture of Danny out front. As they walked along, Dennis noticed children and adults fighting over food from garbage cans. He gripped Danny's hand tighter, thankful that he could take this small boy home.

Just as Dennis started to focus the camera, a guard appeared with a gun. Dennis put the camera down, grabbed Danny, and raced back to the apartment.

That evening Dennis gave Danny a piece of toast and tea and tucked him in bed. Tomorrow would be a long day for him. Dennis returned to finish his dinner and met another American, a man who was in El Salvador repairing computers. He happened to be from Oregon, too.

After Dennis had gone to bed, a huge explosion wakened him suddenly. It sounded like it was next door, and the whole building was illuminated. Frightened, he grabbed Danny and raced outside.

The man from dinner appeared. "What are you doing out here?" he asked.

"They just bombed the building," Dennis said, pointing.

"Hey, that was just thunder, and it was lightning that lit up the building."

A sheepish Dennis went back inside. He was exhausted. He still couldn't believe any of this was happening. Danny finally got back to sleep, then Dennis slipped to his knees beside the bed.

"O, Lord, forgive me. Forgive me for all my doubts and fears."

"What do I have to do?" it seemed like God was saying. "I've done everything. Why do you doubt? I healed your son. I made the trip possible. Why do you keep doubting?"

Dennis knew that from that moment on he had nothing more to worry about. It was a strange but wonderful feeling.

The return flight was scheduled to leave at eight the next morning. For some reason, Dennis woke at 5:30 A.M. He skipped breakfast, and as he paid his bill, he told the host he wanted to go to the airport right then.

"The flight doesn't leave for two more hours."

"I know," Dennis said. "I just want to go now."

At 6:15 A.M. he got a taxi and they arrived at the airport at 6:40. He didn't want to take anymore chances. The ticket counters were open, and he showed them Danny's pass and the other papers.

The ticket agent shook his head. "There is no way we can take him."

"You'd better talk to your supervisor," Dennis said. "These are papers from the American Embassy. They explain why he is coming out on this kind of pass. Believe me, it's okay."

The supervisor came over, looked at the papers, at Dennis, then Danny. After some persuasion and a five-dollar "tip," he said, "I know the American consul's signature— I've seen his handwriting. I'll go ahead and okay it."

So little Danny was going home to America. The last hurdle was over. They boarded the plane, though it wasn't scheduled to leave for another hour. For some reason, the flight was called forty-five minutes ahead of scheduled departure time.

Dennis never did find out why the plane left as early as it did, but he was grateful for the Lord's urging him to get to the airport ahead of time. Dennis and Danny were going *home*!

Chapter Eleven

Heaven's Very Special Child

A meeting was held quite far from earth!
It's time again for another birth.
Said the Angels to the Lord above,
"This Special Child will need much love."

His progress may seem very slow,
Accomplishments he may not show.
And he'll require extra care
From the folks he meets way down there.

He may not run or laugh or play;
His thoughts may seem quite far away.
In many ways he won't adapt
And he'll be known as handicapped.

So let's be careful where he's sent.
We want his life to be content.
Please, Lord, find the parents who
Will do a special job for you.

They will not realize right away
The leading role they're asked to play.

But with this child sent from above
Comes stronger faith and richer love.

And soon they'll know the privilege given
In caring for this gift from Heaven.
Their precious charge so meek and mild
Is Heaven's Very Special child.

                    Edna Massimilla*

It was a picture of a baby named Melissa in the Indiana adoption book that led the Nasons to consider adopting again in early 1977. Diane asked a caseworker for an update on Melissa.

"She's available, but will be difficult to place," the caseworker replied. "Melissa has massive problems, and there's no prognosis for her future." There was a pause. "Would you like me to contact her worker for additional information?"

Diane hesitated. "No, not really, but do keep me informed on her status."

Donny was still a baby, and Diane felt they weren't ready for another child. Apparently the Lord felt otherwise, as Diane couldn't put Melissa out of her mind. The timing didn't seem right, but she didn't always understand His timetable.

The Nasons discussed the possibility of Melissa's "coming home." Wasn't that their vision—working with special children from all parts of the world? They already knew that these children were beautiful in God's sight and could be a real witness for Him.

---

*From *Poems for the Handicapped*. This Is Our Life Publications, P. O. Box 21, Hatboro, PA 19040. Printed with permission.

"It *would* be nice to have a little one Donny's age," Diane said. There was no prognosis, but the Nasons felt strengthened to go ahead. Many of the things they needed could wait, but a child could not. Besides, the Lord knew the prognosis. He knew what He would do in Melissa's life, and it wasn't their place to question. Her picture found a place on the Nasons' crowded bulletin board. The family prayed and, while waiting for her arrival, received additional information on the girl.

Melissa was slow in development. She had myotonic muscular dystrophy, which affected her extremities, and slight cerebral palsy. Following her birth, she'd had a seizure and nearly suffered a stroke. The love of a special foster mother pulled her through the crisis. Melissa also had club feet.

"She'll be a challenge," Diane said, "but I love her already."

Melissa was six months old when she "came home" in July 1977. Everyone loved her on sight, especially Lisa, who was ten and quite the mother's helper.

"Mommy, I'll feed her," Lisa said. "And I can change her, too." Lisa also provided an overabundant amount of love and cuddling.

Feeding Melissa was a real chore. She couldn't swallow, and since the muscles around her mouth didn't work well, the food dribbled back out. When she cried, there was no expression on her face. Tears came to her eyes, and they said it all. In those blue-gray eyes, Diane saw a real fight and determination, and she knew that determination would help Melissa fight many battles.

At first Melissa wore flat shoes with braces and a connecting bar between the shoes. When she raised the contraption up and brought it down with a clunk it really hurt. The braces were a hassle. She had to wear them constantly except at bath time, and she protested strongly. It took several people to hold her and put on the braces tight enough so she couldn't take them off.

Melissa also had to wear a hip pillow, which she detested as much as the braces. She moaned and cried at night until Diane got up and held her. Nothing made her happy until the pillow was removed, but she eventually got used to it.

"I don't like to see her cry," Lori would say. "Does she have to wear the braces *all* the time?"

"Yes," Diane answered. "We have to be tough about things like that. Melissa has a lot to overcome, but she won't get better without a little give on her part and lots of determination on ours."

At eleven months, Melissa rolled over and pushed herself up to a crawling position. It was a great achievement and she beamed. Her arms were stronger, but her legs were weak because of the dystrophy and club feet. At twelve months Melissa pulled herself across the kitchen floor— another milestone.

Melissa got a lot of stimulation from watching "Sesame Street" on TV—the one program Diane allows the children to see.

When Melissa was two, Diane took her to the University of Oregon Medical School for a complete evaluation. All of the reports came back with the same verdict: myotonic muscular dystrophy, a cerebral palsy spasticity, and club feet. No prognosis was given, but it was felt that Melissa wouldn't be very bright, or achieve much. The reports agreed that she needed braces.

The Nasons felt Melissa needed surgery on her feet at that point, because she was determined to walk and tried constantly. All of the specialists consulted wanted to delay the surgery and in the meantime keep her in braces.

"This child needs an operation now," Diane declared to a

doctor at the Shriners Hospital in Portland. "She walks around, holding onto furniture. If she doesn't have braces on, her feet turn under, and she walks on top of them until her ankles bleed."

Six months later when surgery was finally agreed on, Melissa stayed two weeks at the Shriners Hospital, waiting to be scheduled. But the waiting list was long at this institution that offers free services to children who are sponsored by an adult member. Finally Diane said, "No more of this waiting," and took her back home.

Still Melissa was determined to walk.

Since the Nasons would be moving to Sisters soon, Diane decided to take Melissa to a new orthopedic surgeon in Bend.

The doctor looked at Melissa's feet and shook his head. "This is the worst case of club feet I've ever seen."

"I know," Diane replied "I can't get anyone to perform the surgery she needs to enable her to walk."

"I'll schedule it for the end of next week," the surgeon said. "How does that sound?"

"That sounds terrific!" Diane said. At last she had found a doctor who could help Melissa.

Melissa had the surgery and came home the same night with casts up to her hips. She was the center of attention and loved every minute of it.

"Oh, Melissa," Mark said, "can I write my name on your cast?"

"And I'll draw a picture," Lisa added.

The casts didn't stop Melissa. They were heavy, but she still crawled with them and banged them up. She even stood, though her legs and knees were bent. Nothing stopped her determination to walk.

The miracle happened on a Sunday morning before church. Everyone was bustling around, brushing hair, putting on sweaters, looking for Bibles. Suddenly Scott yelled: "Hey! You've got to come here and see this!"

Nasons came from all different directions and there was Melissa, all smiles, eyes sparkling, *walking for the first time.* Everyone clapped and cheered her on.

"Oh, Melissa, you're beautiful!" Diane cried, grabbing her camera and snapping pictures. "I knew you could do it all the time!"

"We're going to be late for church," Scott said, glancing at his watch.

"That's okay," Dennis said. "This celebration is more important."

It was an exciting moment. Doctors and specialists had all said, "Don't expect this child to walk. With her club feet, the dystrophy, the spasticity, and the cerebral palsy, it's not expected."

"Well, they forgot to tell Melissa that," Diane said.

Melissa continued to progress. Donny was a great stimulator, and she tried to keep up with him.

But Melissa's problems weren't over. Diane noticed one day how easily the child was distracted when people were talking. She made an appointment and took Melissa to an audiologist for a hearing test.

"She has a great hearing loss in the right ear, and slight loss in the left," the audiologist said. "That, as well as the dystrophy, explains her somewhat garbled speech."

A hearing specialist was recommended, and two weeks later Melissa had tubes surgically inserted in her ears. When her hearing was tested a few months later, it was nearly perfect.

An Easter Seals therapist who examined Melissa on one occasion was astounded at her progress. "I could suggest a few exercises, but the stimulation of her family and what you've done is amazing. There's not much else I can offer."

"We started from the feet up," Diane told a friend, "and now we'll work on Melissa's speech."

The Lord worked that out too. The speech therapist who taught at the elementary school in Sisters agreed to come by the Nasons' house and tutor Melissa on a private basis.

Melissa was also fitted with glasses, something she detested. She started playing a game of "Hide the glasses." No amount of coaxing would make her tell. Then Diane discovered Melissa's favorite spot behind the bed, and the glasses were found, to Melissa's dismay.

Potty training was another area of difficulty, as it is with most spastic children. It remains frustrating to the older girls, who help change Melissa. It bothers Melissa too, as she loves her family and wants nothing more than to please them. As Melissa gains better muscle control, Diane hopes for more success.

Sometimes the days are long for Melissa, and on those days Diane says she wouldn't advocate adoption of a handicapped child to just anyone.

"People must be totally committed and convinced about what they are doing to take a child like Melissa. They have to be open to what the Lord can do in the lives of children and in their own lives."

Melissa enriches everyone, as any handicapped child can do. Caring for a handicapped child can add an amazing depth and understanding to a family unit.

"Our home-grown little ones get a lot of pleasure in things other children their age wouldn't," Diane adds. "They rejoice in watching Melissa get up and walk. They get excited about accomplishments, and that's good for them. They are learning that God made none of us perfect, and that He gave us individuality and our own will to do whatever He wants us to do. Some of these little ones are our greatest ambassadors. They reach out and touch people without really trying, just by being themselves. So much love shines through, and since God is love, we're talking about the same thing."

What are the expectations for Melissa?

"We don't have any," Diane said. "We don't stand there and say 'just because she is four years old she has to be potty-trained.' That would be nice and certainly easier, but that is not where Melissa is right now."

It would be easier, too, if Melissa could dress herself, but she isn't coordinated. Still, she tries. One day she managed to get on six pairs of underpants—all at the same time. They weren't hers, and she knew it, but it was so much fun putting on bigger underwear!

Some say that Melissa is lucky to have a family such as the Nasons to adopt her. Diane disagrees. "We're the lucky ones. Lucky to be able to receive all that Melissa can give and to share it with other people. We are blessed to have Melissa as part of our family."

As the Nasons reached out to children with various handicaps, they set down some guidelines. Many of their co-workers in adoptions had come to the same conclusions, and they decided to share them with other agencies.

In the past, handicapped children have been unadoptable: no effort was made to place them. The decision to adopt a handicapped child leads to strength for creativity and purpose in the child's life. It ultimately affects an entire family in the same way.

Some of the conclusions about this type of adoption are based on fear, especially fear of the unknown. If one erases the unknowns and replaces them with the creativity of God, then there are no restrictions. Only then can reason and vision become clear. When adoptive parents achieve that realization they dismiss their fears and believe what God can do in the life of their child.

Many people, when confronting a handicapped child, see the handicaps and not the child. But people should look at the child in a different light, bypassing the physical deformities to consider a child with a unique personality, who *just happens to have a handicap.*

The personality has to come first, and this is difficult, as Diane has found. Often, parents are obsessed with the handicap and wonder what it will do to the family. How can the family endure it, and will they have to give up all the things that they really like doing? they wonder. Or how can the family of above average intelligence slow down for mental handicaps? The world is geared to above-average achievement and high-level entertainment. Fear of the child's handicap has to be erased, Diane stresses. The focus should be on the family unit, which should work cooperatively with a purpose.

In September 1977, the Nasons embarked on another adoption that was complicated and would affect the lives of each member of the family. The child named Mandy arrived with shigella, as mentioned earlier, but her handicap was more serious.

Ann Scott, from PLAN Adoption Agency in McMinnville, called Diane one evening with exciting news. "We've received some information about a baby girl in India. I couldn't think of anyone who would be more open to this child with her type of handicap."

"What's the handicap?" Diane asked, not realizing it was different from any she had encountered before.

"This little girl has no arms. She's now in one of Mother Theresa's orphanages and is very special to her. She appears to have a high intellect and lots of potential. Mother Theresa doesn't want her to spend the rest of her life in an orphanage, but if they can't find the right home, she'll be taken care of by the Sisters."

Diane's mind whirled. This little girl would certainly be

a challenge. She'd had experience with cerebral palsy, asthma, muscular dystrophy, emotional problems, and slow learners—but no arms?

"How did it happen?" she asked.

"Seems the pregnancy was untimely, so the mother took some kind of medication to abort the baby and it failed."

"Wow!" Diane said. "I'll have to see what Dennis thinks."

"One more thing," Ann went on. "These adoptions from India are not easy. There's lots of paperwork, and it takes a good dose of perseverance. That's another reason I thought of you. I knew you'd stick with it and get this little girl out of India and to a real family."

There was immediate opposition from family members not living in the Nason home.

"No arms—that's a *real* handicap."

"She'll be a burden."

"Diane, don't do this," her mother pleaded. She was concerned about Diane's health. She took Dennis aside to say, "Please don't adopt this child."

But there was positive feedback from coworkers in adoption and from many Christian friends.

"You can do it—we know you can."

"Look at how you handled Melissa."

"How can you say no?"

Children in the immediate family circle were supportive. "We'll help," they said. "You can count on us."

The Nasons were in complete agreement: The Lord wanted them to "bring this child home." So they proceeded.

Diane had been warned that the paperwork was endless, but she was not prepared for the myriad documents which had to be done in a precise way. "I'd helped countless people with overseas adoptions, but this was ridiculous," she stated.

The adoption had to be approved by the Indian consul in

San Francisco, and they needed five copies of everything. All papers had to be notarized by a state notary. Another big problem was the advance parole. The Nasons had already obtained one special advance parole beyond the usual allotment of two visas to get Danny out of El Salvador. Now they were trying for an advance parole on medical grounds. (In 1980 the limit on the number of children from overseas who could be adopted was lifted.)

Diane started a letter to the consul who had to approve the adoption.

> We know this little girl is our child, and we love her already. We can hardly wait to include her within the love and security of our family. We have contacted doctors in our area to facilitate the treatment and to fit her with artificial arms. The opportunities are endless in our area. Many specialists are available and are already anticipating her arrival. Please help us to bring our little girl home. We would appreciate so very much if you could stamp the enclosed documents for us. Each separate document has to be stamped and verified, or the judge in India won't accept them.
>
> We want our documents to be totally correct so no time will be lost. Enclosed you will find the total fee required to validate each document and a self-addressed, stamped folder to send the documents back to us as soon as possible. Thank you so much for your concern for the children of India.

The documents were returned, stamped and in order. Kathy, a representative from Mother Theresa's orphanage, couldn't believe it. "What did you do to him?"

Diane laughed. "I zapped him with a little prayer."

The parole visa which had been approved at the district level, then by the regional director, was denied by the immigration director in Washington, D.C.

"Why?" the Nasons asked. "It was approved at all levels. Why are you denying it?"

"Because this child is too handicapped and will become a burden," was the official answer.

"We're not ready to accept that," Diane argued. "We'll go to bat for her. She has a bright mind. I'm sure she can get along just fine without her arms."

Again, both Oregon senators, Mark Hatfield and Bob Packwood, got involved. It took a lot of requests from different people, but finally the Immigration Service granted the special visa. They realized that this little girl could make a contribution to American society, something which the Nasons never doubted.

The next big hurdle was finances, but, as in the past, the money came miraculously. The Easthill Church in Gresham, Oregon, heard about the problem of getting Mandy out of India and took up a love offering to pay for travel expenses. A sponsor was found who would go over and bring Mandy and two other children to America.

Two more people would play a large part in Mandy's life before she finally arrived in the States. She had a convulsion on the airplane and had to be left behind in Hawaii. A doctor took her into his home and nursed her back to health, after diagnosing shigella, the bloody diarrhea condition. When Mandy was finally well, a stewardess offered to bring Mandy home on her own time.

Six months after Diane had started everything rolling, Mandy, now eleven months old, was "home."

When Mandy arrived in March 1978, she had three plastic bracelets from India around her ankles. She played with the bracelets constantly, passing them from toe to toe. She could stretch a rubber band with her toes. Diane suspected Mandy could compensate for not having arms because her toes were so dexterous. They were long and slender, like fingers. God had given her in the place of arms the ability to use her feet.

Diane encouraged Mandy to play and told the other children not to pass her things, that she should learn to fend for herself. That was the start of a long battle to make Mandy help herself. *Handicapped children have to be encouraged to help themselves*, Diane feels.

The first obstacle to overcome was eating. Diane fed Mandy until she was about one and a half, then said, "Okay, Mandy. You aren't a baby anymore. Let's see what you can do for yourself. Just go at it."

She refused. She liked being fed plus all the attention that went with it.

Diane finally said, "I'm sorry, Mandy, but you're not going to be able to eat if you don't feed yourself."

Mandy didn't believe Diane and sat through five meals without being fed. She cried, "I can't do it."

"Yes, you can, Mandy. Take your toes like we showed you. Use the spoon and pick up your food."

After looking around at everyone who was eating, she picked up the spoon and started eating. She was clumsy at first and spilled food, but she learned to feed herself. Everyone cheered and clapped.

The next obstacle was walking. That took three months and was difficult, because at first Mandy had no balance. It was terrifying because when she fell, she landed right on her face. She had no arms to break her fall. *But she had to learn.*

Diane tried putting her in a walker, but Mandy fell through the bottom; babies use their arms to maintain balance in a walker. The older girls held their arms out hour after hour, and finally Mandy walked two steps, then three steps, but always with the knowledge that her sisters would catch her.

Diane knew Mandy could do it, but a mixture of fear and stubbornness kept her from trying. She had to overcome it. Diane repeated constantly, "Mandy, you can do it. *You can do it.*"

After a frustrating time of not getting anywhere, Diane finally resorted to food again to encourage Mandy to try walking. She fixed Mandy's plate and left it sitting on the table across the room from Mandy. It took three meals that time. At the end of the third meal, she looked at Diane.

"All right," Mandy said, standing up and walking over all by herself and plopping down to eat.

"*Yeah, Mandy!*" they all yelled. "We knew you could do it!"

Mandy seemed to resent being taken away from the only security she had ever known—the Sisters at the orphanage in India. For a whole year after she arrived, she wouldn't call Diane "Mommy." Although she accepted Diane in the role of mother, she also resented her.

One morning when Diane was getting breakfast, Mandy looked up with those huge brown eyes and said, "You're my Mommy."

A lump came to Diane's throat. "Mandy, do you really mean that?"

She nodded. "Yes, you're my Mommy."

Oh, thank You, Lord, for small favors, Diane thought. *I really needed to hear that just now.*

Mandy was such a charmer. Wherever the Nasons took her, people would stop and say "Poor little thing," which was exactly what she didn't need. She needed to be appreciated for her accomplishments and what she *could* do— not for being a "poor little thing."

"People tend to oversympathize," Diane feels. "It's a natural reaction, but when you're working with handicapped children, it's not what they need."

Mandy's biggest game with any member of the family was "I don't have any arms. I can't do that."

The kids never gave her a minute of sympathy. "So, you don't have any arms. So what? You can get your own book. You go ask Mom for a drink of water."

She did need to be lifted up to be able to stick her cup under the faucet. Drinking from a cup took practice too. It takes a lot of balance, but Diane knew she could do it. She'd fill Mandy's plastic cup only half full. She learned well and seldom spilled.

"She takes her little toe, usually on her left foot, and, by using her right knee to support the cup, picks it up with her toes and then drinks," Diane explained.

Mandy is required to take her silverware and cup to the kitchen after she eats. Doesn't everyone else in the family? She picks up the handle of her cup with her teeth and takes it in to be washed, then makes another trip with her silverware. She also brings her plate, tucked under her chin.

When the Nasons were in New York to receive an award from the Odyssey Foundation, Mandy met the top orthopedic surgeon for children at Rusk Institute. He took one look at Mandy and said, "She is very intelligent, isn't she?"

"Yes," Diane answered. "She certainly is."

"I see no reason why she couldn't be fitted with an electronic implant for *electronic arms*. That might work better than the artificial arms, because she might not resent it as much."

"That sounds super," Diane said.

It was a thrilling moment for the Nasons when Lisa came home from junior high with a picture in a children's magazine circulated monthly to all the schools in the United States. The article was about Mother Theresa winning the Nobel Peace Prize, and the picture showed her holding an armless baby. It was Mandy.

In 1978, while Diane was waiting for Mandy to 'come home,' she had been contacted by a caseworker at the Sheltering Arms Agency in New York.

"Mrs. Nason, didn't you inquire about a baby boy a while back?" Susan asked.

"Yes, I did," Diane responded.

In October 1976, Diane had contacted the adoption exchange in New York and asked for the status of twenty children to share with interested people. One of those was a seven-month-old, multiracial boy. She had pinned his picture on the bulletin board and had prayed for him all this time.

"Several people have turned down the child," the caseworker continued. "The prognosis for his learning abilities is not good since the drugs taken by the biological mother may affect him considerably. Also, he has a slight case of cerebral palsy on his left side, but he's a beautiful little boy. Are you still interested?"

Dennis and Diane discussed it at length. Donny would be a great pal for this little guy. Yes, they'd adopt him into their hearts and home.

The agency sent the airplane ticket, and the day before Saint Patrick's Day, 1978, Dennis flew to New York to pick up David Lee Nason.

Dennis met Mrs. Boyd, director of the agency. A poised, gentle, beautiful black woman, she works hard at uniting *her* children with the right family.

The following day Dennis flew back with the small boy. As the plane landed in Medford, Dennis came down the steps with David in his arms. The big brown eyes stared at the sixteen pairs of eyes smiling at him. "Welcome home, David," they yelled in unison. He smiled back. He was home.

Chapter Twelve

Needs of the Older Child

"**P**lacing the older child is one of our main concerns here at Albertina Kerr Center for Children," says Herbert Hansen, program director. "Beginning in 1970, fewer babies were available for adoption, and more families were interested in adopting. We began to ask if they would be interested in a child as old as three. More recently," he went on, "the age of waiting children has changed. Our greatest need now is placing the child who is ten, eleven, or twelve years of age."

The Nasons knew about the needs of the older child. They have adopted children who were ten, eleven, fourteen, fifteen, and seventeen years of age. Gary was seventeen when he "came home."

They had heard about Gary through the Northwest Adoption Exchange, a newly formed group. The coordinator of the group was the keynote speaker at an adoption conference Diane had planned and organized. Heads of various agencies were invited, and the turnout was greater than expected. Everyone seemed to have the same purpose: to help children who needed to be adopted.

The speaker had prepared a book on hard-to-place children in the Northwest and brought slides of children waiting for adoption within the area.

Gary was an alcohol-syndrome child. His mother had been an alcoholic and had given birth to several children by different fathers, but she had no way to take care of her children. She died of alcoholism shortly after the youngest child was born. She had passed the alcohol-syndrome tendency on to Gary and his fifteen-year-old sister, Kim. An alcohol-syndrome child tends to be either retarded or slow to develop, and is able to achieve only to a certain level. No one knows where that level is, because it depends on the amount of prenatal damage.

Gary was progressing slowly; Kim was moderately retarded. But both functioned well and were capable of becoming independent adults.

"The reason I want to find a home for Gary and Kim is because each time I see Gary, he asks, 'Why can't I have a home? What's *wrong* with me? Doesn't *anyone* want to adopt me?'" the coordinator said, shaking her head. "It really gets to you—you know?"

"Yes," Diane said in agreement. "There're lots of kids like that."

"The main problems with Gary are his age, his Indian/ white parentage, and his learning level," the speaker went on.

The story touched Dennis and Diane's hearts.

"We could take both Gary and his sister, Kim, if we didn't have this problem with the state about our home study," Diane said.

"Listen, why don't I talk to your agency representative tomorrow at the conference?" the coordinator suggested. "Maybe they'll agree to do it."

She spoke to the agency, putting them on the spot. "Well, sure, of course, we'll be glad to work with you and the Nasons," they replied.

Gary and Kim lived in different foster homes, and when Gary heard they were going to be adopted, he could hardly believe it.

The Nasons later discovered that Kim wasn't as eager about the adoption, but Gary had talked her into it. At that age, children can make their own decision about being adopted. In another year Gary would technically be on his own, but due to his slow development and having three years of school left, he wouldn't be independent for quite some time.

Gary and Kim arrived in January 1978.

The Nason household rang with excitement as they got ready for their new brother and sister.

Older teenagers are among the most difficult adoptions because they are set in their ways—especially those who have been in foster care for several years. Gary and Kim had known nothing but foster homes since their birth.

Gary fit in immediately. He grabbed Dennis and Diane and hugged them hard. "I'm so glad to have a mom and dad," he said. "I *love* you. I always wanted a mom and dad to come home to when I'm out on my own."

"He's so sensitive and caring," Diane said to Dennis later. "Did you notice how the kids loved him from the first?"

"Yes," Dennis answered. "And I noticed him pitching in and helping with the little ones."

"He's a beautiful addition to our family," Diane said. "Now Kim—she's different." (They soon discovered how different.)

Gary was working at the sixth grade level in most of his studies, though he was almost a junior in high school. The kids teased him because he was slow, but he had learned to live with that, and his personality helped him rise above it in various situations.

The teachers liked Gary because he cooperated and was eager to please. All reports indicated that he would never graduate from high school because he couldn't catch up. But maybe, if he stayed in school for another ten years or so. . . .

"I don't believe that," Diane said. "Gary has the will to succeed, and now that he has the permanency of a home, his whole world is opening up."

The Nasons had heard about Gary's previous problem with an ulcer, but they didn't realize how serious it was. Nine months after he arrived, his ulcer perforated, requiring surgery.

"That ulcer began three years ago," Diane told Dennis. "I bet all that lying awake and worrying about not having a family started it."

"Mom, don't leave me," Gary begged Diane as he clung to her hand from his hospital bed. "I'm so scared."

Diane stayed at his side.

Gary was out of school for three weeks. It was difficult, as he wanted to graduate more than anything, and now he was even more behind.

A second surgery was scheduled, but Diane questioned the need for it. It would be an extensive operation and would restrict Gary's eating ability for the rest of his life.

"We're going to pray about it," Diane told the doctor. "We don't feel he'll need the surgery."

"All right," the doctor said, "but I advise that he have it, the sooner the better."

Gary felt the way the Nasons did, so the operation was put off. And miraculously, Gary continued to improve. The Lord knew this was one boy who'd had enough, and answered everyone's prayers.

One afternoon, Gary came home in tears. "Mom, they told me I couldn't graduate."

"You just hang in there," Diane said. "You're going to graduate, I know you will."

It was still six months before graduation. Diane maintained there was a way. Infuriated, she marched over to the school and spoke to the teacher who had given Gary the bad news. "I don't want you teaching my son," she declared. "Just stay away from him. Gary *is* going to get a diploma. Period."

She spoke to the assistant principal, explaining the situation, and asked him to intervene and put Gary in another classroom. A dean of boys was selected to work with Gary on his program so he could get enough credits.

"You never stop fighting for your children's rights," Diane maintains. "When you know you're right, and if you're in tune with the Lord and you've prayed about it, then I say go to bat for whatever cause you believe in."

This *was* a cause. Gary's diploma would affect him the rest of his life. The Nasons' stand didn't make them popular with the school's special education department, but they won. Gary got his diploma.

Afterward, he rushed up to Diane and gave her a big kiss. "I did it, Mom! I really did it!"

"I never had any doubt," Diane replied.

They bought him a cake and had a big celebration.

Gary wanted to learn to be independent. "I think I'd like to get a job, have my own place," he said.

"How about cooking?" Dennis asked, remembering the times Gary hung around when he was cooking.

"I don't know if I'd be able to get all the orders right."

"Why not start a little lower and work your way up?" Diane suggested. "When your dad was in school, he worked as a dishwasher."

Dennis spoke to the owner of the local restaurant. He explained Gary's problem areas and asked if he might work there. "He's a dandy worker and helped out in the cafeteria at school. He needs a little leeway and some learning experiences."

The owner was enthusiastic. "I have a hard time finding good, steady help. I'll be glad to work with your son."

The Nasons helped Gary with the first month's rent on a small furnished apartment. Diane found some old camping dishes, pots and pans, and Gary already had the black and white TV they'd given him for a graduation present. Next Diane took him to the grocery, showed him how to shop for sale items, and pointed out more nutritional items. Gary now buys all his food, pays his rent by himself, and has opened his own bank account.

"He's so proud," Diane said, her face beaming. "Just as we're proud of his many accomplishments. He stops by the post office often to see his dad and comes out to the farm to visit. He accepted the Lord right after coming to us and enjoys attending church each Sunday."

This from a boy who wasn't supposed to be on his own or graduate from high school. He had the will and desire to persevere against incredible odds. Gary stands as an example for older children who have handicaps.

All of this was possible because a certain boy kept saying, year after year, over and over again, *What's wrong with me? Why can't I have a family?*

Though adoption workers agree that the ideal situation is for every child to become part of a family unit, it doesn't always work out, especially in the case of older children. They have adapted to a certain lifestyle, and often resist change.

Since most foster homes are not permanent, the foster

child may experience more freedom than a child in a conventional family setting. Consequently, there is a point in the life of a child when it is too late for adoption. Even as a teenager Gary needed to belong to a family; Kim did not.

Since Kim had never been an integral part of a family unit and had relied on having the caseworker never more than a phone call away, she resisted learning to do things for herself.

Diane tried to interest Kim in 4-H work, but the animals frightened her. Diane attempted to teach her cooking, but Kim didn't seem to understand the importance of following safety instructions when using the stove. *Surely, she'll feel a closeness with one of the little ones,* Diane thought. Most adopted children felt the bonding immediately, but Kim remained aloof.

Kim begged to return to her former foster home in Washington.

"Kim, that's impossible," Diane said, putting an arm around her. "We've adopted you. You're our daughter now. You're a Nason."

"But, I don't like it here."

Gary couldn't understand. "Kim, I *love* having a mom and dad. Why aren't *you* happy?"

Kim ran away several times, but was picked up and brought back.

"Kim," Diane said one day, "when you're eighteen, if you still want to return to Washington, I'll buy the ticket and see that you get there."

Kim didn't want to wait. After running away again, she ended up in another state, and is now enrolled in a special school with constant individual care.

Kim called Diane a few days before her eighteenth birthday. "Mom," she said, "I just want you to know I'm in adult foster care now [a sheltered environment]. Oh, and Mom, I go to church every Sunday."

"Kim was one child who shouldn't have been submitted for adoption at age fifteen," Diane concluded. "We learned that not all children are able to adjust to a family situation."

In 1980, the Sheltering Arms Agency in New York called Diane with a desperate need.

"We have an immature child of fourteen who has emotional problems and brain damage. The boy can function, is capable of learning and can be part of a family. He must be removed from his present family situation," the caseworker explained. "He was scheduled as an adoptive placement, but the mother decided there was too much competition with the other child in the house and they didn't want Jeff after all."

Dennis and Diane had six teenagers now and questioned their desire for another in their home. They feel strongly that teens take almost a one-to-one commitment, like preschoolers.

They learned that Jeff had been in foster care all his life. His parents had a background of alcoholism and drug use, but he had been close to others with artistic talent and who had gone on to higher educaton. Jeff was a victim of his past.

After repeated attempts at foster placement, and due to lack of a better facility, Jeff was placed in a mental institution for evaluation. While there, he was physically and emotionally abused. When the abuse was discovered he was removed immediately, but the damage had been done.

The Sheltering Arms Agency felt that the Nasons could handle Jeff because of their expertise in dealing with various emotional problems. They felt that Jeff could relate to some of the other children if he couldn't relate at first to the adults.

"Of course, we have a problem with the home study," Diane said.

"Yes, we know, but what about the agency you worked with in the adoption of Melissa?"

"That's a possibility," Diane said. "They've expanded their adoption work and probably would do it."

The agency agreed to pay all expenses, and in January 1980, Jeff flew to Oregon with his caseworker.

Jeff looked ten, not fourteen. He was tiny, wore horn-rimmed glasses and talked incessantly. He had never had a mom, dad, or siblings, so he didn't know how to act around other children. He displayed his brain dysfunction when he became upset at not knowing how to handle situations.

Jeff had been told not to hit or spank any of the children, but one afternoon David suddenly cried out. Diane hurried into the room to find Jeff with a toy truck, going bong, bong, bong on David's head.

"What are you doing?" Diane demanded.

"He wouldn't stop crying."

"How would you like someone to hit you on the head, then tell you to quit crying while he kept beating you?"

"I didn't think of that."

"Well," Diane replied, "suppose you sit in your room and think about it. The next time you'll get a spanking because you're acting like a two-year-old."

Jeff was tested and enrolled in special education classes in all subjects except art. One teacher made Jeff especially uneasy with her frequent, prying questions.

"Well, Jeff," she'd say, "what's going on in your family today? How's Mandy?"

Diane did what she could to stop what seemed to be

unnecessary meddling. Jeff didn't need extra tension at school. He needed security and acceptance at every level.

Jeff also felt he was picked on in school because of his size. School wasn't the right place for him, not when he needed good, solid family strokes. Shortly afterward the Nasons obtained permission to have their high-school-age children take correspondence courses at home through the Alpha Omega Christian Program.

Jeff also had the problem of many older children available for adoption. He had never had any previous supervision or been given rules to follow. He ate when and what he wanted. He had never been required to perform chores or be responsible for any particular activity. Suddenly he had a job that everyone relied on him to do.

There were days when Jeff thought, *If I don't make my bed or empty the trash, someone else will do it.*

"This is a family, Jeff," Diane explained. "Families help each other and do things for the benefit of all. It can't be any different for you."

With most children of this age and background, family gatherings, holiday times, or birthdays create upsetting and disruptive activities. These occasions bring back too many memories of unhappy birthdays or missed celebrations, and the children don't know how to handle it.

On Thanksgiving Jeff hit Kecia because she was bothering him. Hitting girls is forbidden—in fact, the Nasons don't allow hitting at all. The time to be disciplined was then, holiday or not. Jeff got a spanking and was sent to his room without dessert.

That was when Jeff decided to run away to New York. A neighbor picked him up on the way to Bend. He stopped to call the Nasons, turned around, and Jeff was gone. Jeff ended up in the shoe store where Mark worked. Mark held onto him and called his parents.

"I won't do that again," Jeff said when Dennis picked him up. "Nobody cares about me out there, and that was frightening."

Each day is an unknown entity with Jeff. He's unpredictable. But he is learning, learning what a family means, and what it means to have brothers and sisters who will stand up for you and care about you. He's also learning to deal with the younger children on a rational level.

Jeff later drew a huge red apple and put it on the refrigerator. "This is the best apple I've ever drawn," it read. "I want you to have it. I'm so glad you adopted me. Thank you for making my adoption final. Your son, Jeff."

Jeff had seen his new birth certificate for the first time, and it meant a lot to him. He was a Nason, and no one was going to send him away no matter what he did. He was there to stay.

Jeff knows the Lord. That may be his salvation in the earthly sense of the word as well as the heavenly. He's accepted in the youth group, which means a lot to him after being ridiculed and downgraded for so long. He craves love and acceptance.

Dealing with this type of child takes a different kind of commitment. It's not an easy adoption. No adoption is easy when you are dealing with retardation or an emotional problem. Dennis and Diane feel the Lord sent them Jeff so that they would know how to help others work with brain-damaged children.

In November 1981, Mrs. Boyd, director of the Sheltering Arms Agency, called again.

"Diane, I know you've just finalized Jeff's adoption, but I wondered how you felt about taking more children. We have twins, black/white, a boy and a girl, ten years old. They really need a home. They haven't attended school this past fall because they've been moved around so much. The twins come from Harlem."

"Yes," Diane responded, "I'm definitely interested. Send us some more information. We'll pray about it and call you back."

They prayed and talked it over with the children. The children were open to their needs and wanted to accept the twins into their family.

Dorell, the girl, had some learning problems. Danny was at grade level. Herb, their caseworker, reviewed the material on the children and updated the Nasons' home study.

Diane caught her breath at her first glimpse of the twins when they arrived at the airport in December. They were beautiful, with medium-brown skin and long eyelashes. Dorell had lightly curled, medium-brown hair. Darin (his new name since they already had a Danny) had tightly curled black hair.

Dorell had an even temperament and became a contributing member of the family soon after she came. She helped with the little ones and the laundry. Her schoolwork needed immediate help, but she tried so hard to please everyone.

Diane had Dorell's hair cut short, and the new style with soft waves really set her off.

"She's a knockout," Dennis exclaimed. "Looks like Donna Summer."

"Yes," Diane agreed, "when the Lord handpicks, He does a good job, doesn't He?"

Darin, being the opposite, displayed a few problems at first. He was testing to see if this was going to be his permanent home, testing to see if the Nasons loved him enough to discipline him and would still love him after he behaved badly.

He threw temper tantrums at school. The teacher asked Darin to do something that he didn't want to. When he was sent to the principal's office, he started kicking the door.

The Nasons were summoned. Both arrived at school, spanked Darin, then talked to him.

"Darin, we've had a few too many of these episodes at school. We told you if you did it again, we were going to come down here and deal with you right here. You're not coming home just because you have a problem. You're going to face it at school."

Darin went back to his classroom and apologized to the class.

Dennis reaffirmed their position. "Next time you pull this, Darin, you're going to get your paddling in front of the class, and that will be embarrassing."

The tantrums stopped, but he misbehaved in other ways.

Accustomed to getting free food, especially hot lunch at school, Darin made eating a focal point in his life. He conned one boy into buying his lunch the first couple of days. When Diane discovered this, she made Darin pay the boy back. He also ate his lunch before arriving at school, then told his teacher he needed a hot lunch because he was *so* hungry.

Diane called the school. "No way are you to give him a hot lunch. He has to learn self-discipline."

And there was a problem on the bus. "Dennis," the bus driver said one day, "Darin threw a fit on the bus and became disruptive. Your daughter, Lori, sat on him to calm him down. Could you talk to him?"

"I'll do better than that," Dennis answered. "Since it's Friday, Darin will be at the bus stop at 7 A.M. Monday morning with something to say to you."

On Monday Dennis, Darin, and the Ping-Pong paddle went to the bus stop.

"You'll give this to the bus driver, Darin, and tell him how sorry you are and apologize to the kids on the bus. You'll sit right behind the bus driver from now on."

"If Darin misbehaves again," Dennis told the driver and the hushed crowd of kids, "You are to use this in front of everyone."

"Dennis," the bus driver confided later, "That did so much good for my whole bus. I appreciate that a lot."

Darin hasn't created a problem on the bus since.

Darin is a bright boy, which meant he kept thinking of ways to misbehave, but slowly and surely the old ways are going. He has much potential to mold and guide.

"Persistence and total commitment is the answer. And prayer," Diane feels.

Love and discipline went hand in hand to make one boy a useful vessel for the Lord.

Candy Wheeler, in her book, *Adopting Older Children*, explains that a child who has known continued rejection and insecurity will expect to be rejected again, and perhaps even provoke rejection.

The older child is a "challenge" child. One must realize that older children are literally survivors. They may have problems relating to school, stealing, lying, running away, foul language, bed-wetting, foster parents, and sibling separation.

Proverbs 21:21 says, "He who follows righteousness and mercy finds life, righteousness, and honor."

Chapter Thirteen

Role Model Children

Is there an advantage to raising biological children and adopted children together?

The Nasons believe you have the best of the two worlds when you have both "home-grown" kids and adopted children.

"When you work with children with various handicaps, you discover they need to relate to normally developing children," Diane states. Donny is the role model child for the preschool children, especially those with coordination problems, such as Mandy with no arms, Melissa with muscular dystrophy, and David with learning defects.

"I remember when Donny would run outside to play, climbing on the swing set and going down the slide," Diane recalls. "Mandy watched from the sidelines, her big brown eyes taking in every move. Could she try to come down the slide? Oh, but it looked scary. I could have rushed outside and coaxed her, 'C'mon, Mandy you can do it, you *know* you can,' but it wouldn't have worked as well," Diane said. "By watching Donny, she finally tried it. If you don't think this is an accomplishment, remember how much you use your arms to balance yourself in coming down a slide."

Who was on the sidelines cheering her on, clapping and praising her? Donny, of course.

Some mornings Diane has a class in physical fitness for the little ones. They do simple things like turning somersaults, skipping, hopping, jumping. The children try, but they learn much quicker from Donny. And the youngest home-grown girl, Diana, is also there, encouraging the little ones.

"It was all part of God's plan, though we didn't know it then," Diane said. "He knew we needed some normal children along with the handicapped. We needed to see normal progress; they needed to have a role model, and that is what the home-grown children are."

Mark was the leader, the beginning. His life had a purpose. If it hadn't been for Mark's severe allergies, Dennis and Diane wouldn't have developed the ability to cope with various illnesses and handicaps.

All of this went through Diane's mind when her handsome six-foot-two-inch son stood by his beautiful bride, Terri, as they recited their marriage vows. He was healthy, robust. On his right stood his best man, Dr. Bill Miller.

"Mark is a pacesetter," Diane explained. "He helped so much with Bill when he lived here. He made Bill try so much more to achieve goals, to go out for sports, to do better in school."

With Gary it worked the same way. Gary, needed to belong to a family, wanted a brother, and looked up to Mark, though Mark was younger. Gary, with a learning disability and appreciative of any help he received, made Mark want to work with him.

Mark was also an example to his younger biological brother, Donny. Donny needed someone to look up to, to pattern himself after. The two boys have a special closeness.

Then came Scott. Scott, totally healthy, helped raise cattle for 4-H. He filled the need for a model in caring for animals and farm work which Mark couldn't do because of his severe asthma problem. Scott helped Lori with her baby pigs. Later when Jeff was adopted, the cows were the main thing he threw his energy into. Jeff rises at 5:30 A.M. to help Scott—the Scott who became a businessman at age twelve.

"Okay, Mom and Dad, if I provide you with milk, can I take the rest of the milk and sell it? I'll pay for the feed out of the profits, and you provide the hay." There were two cows by then.

"Sounds like a winner," Dennis and Diane agreed. "But you'll have to be dedicated. It'll be a night and morning thing. Milkers don't have vacations."

"I know," Scott said. "That's what I want to do."

Up to that point everyone had taken turns milking, but after Scott took charge—he'd made a commitment—it was his job. The milk business grew, with neighbors and friends coming to buy milk. The profit was good, and soon Scott wanted another cow.

"We don't have the money," his parents said. "We'd give it to you, if we had it."

"Well," Scott said, hesitating for a moment, "I think I'll go down to the bank and talk to the manager."

The Nasons admired their son's resourcefulness, but, after all, he was only a twelve-year-old kid. "I hope they don't laugh at him," Diane said.

Bob Bernard was a good friend and associate in financial matters for the Nasons. Often they'd gone into the bank to request a loan. "We're going to adopt another child, and we need five hundred dollars."

They introduced Scott to Bob and waited while their usually shy, withdrawn son explained his proposal.

"I need another cow, Mr. Bernard," Scott announced boldly. "I want to go into the milk business."

"How much do you need?" the older man asked.

"I have a cow lined up, but she'll cost $600," Scott answered.

"That's a lot of money. Tell you what. Go home, write down in black and white what the feed will cost, how much you'll bring in—the whole bit."

They went home, and Dennis helped Scott figure it out.

Scott got the loan. He made his payments, which had been figured into the budget. As a seventh grader, he was in business for himself. From then on, Scott bought all his clothes, paid for his entertainment, and was in control of his life.

The man who had the cow for sale was also going out of business and offered to sell Scott his milking machines and refrigerator.

"I don't have any money," Scott said.

"How much could you pay me each month?" he asked.

"Let's see," Scott said as he figured on a piece of paper. "How about fifty dollars a month?"

"Sounds good to me," the farmer said. "I'll even come out and help you get set up."

Scott remodeled the barn in his spare time. Grandpa Fehlman, a teacher, also knew about electrical wiring, plumbing, and building. He taught Scott and Mark all he knew and helped Dennis with an addition to the three-bedroom house in Ashland.

In 1978, Scott paid off his first loan and asked for another. "I need a producing cow for eight hundred dollars," he explained to the loan officer.

After getting a loan, he built up his herd and the number of milk customers. Besides raising pigs as a 4-H project,

Scott studied veterinary science and received ribbons at the fair. Richard Hill, a local veterinarian, took an interest in Scott and worked with him at no cost. He helped Scott put a cast on a cat's leg, and later helped him with the cows.

Scott also played a major role when the family moved from Ashland to Sisters.

Dennis had spent a year in intensive training for the postmaster's position. "If I get this job, it will be a raise in pay, plus more responsibility," he explained.

"How many are applying for the position in Sisters?"

"About two hundred."

Dennis realized his chances were slim, but he knew if the Lord wanted him to have the job, he'd get it. When he was selected to fill the position and left for Sisters, it meant leaving Diane at home with eighteen kids. A month later, he sent for Scott. Scott got a job on a dairy—milking, cutting and baling hay. It was good experience, but now Diane was left behind with seventeen kids and the house to run. Four months later, Dennis finally located a home suitable for the whole family.

Lisa, the third biological child and first daughter, has always been a help, a real joy. When Lisa was seven, Kari "came home" from Vietnam. Kari, with her many handicaps, enthralled Lisa. From then on, Lisa knew she wanted to work with children perhaps in a youth ministry.

"Lisa never had a problem with any of the children coming into the home," Diane noted. "She always helped and took on the 'second mother' role."

During the Nasons' work with bringing children from Vietnam over for adoption, their telephone rang constantly. Lisa took messages and made sure her parents got each one and the name of the caller.

Lisa's interest in adoptions has developed into a special

understanding of the problems of the children and the situations they were in. She helped sort pictures in the adoption books and still updates the books and takes information on the phone.

Lisa was enthusiastic about 4-H. Home Economics was her real interest, and child development activities intrigued her. In 1978 she made a felt ABC wall hanging. Individual stuffed animals and objects went into each pocket, which represented an alphabet letter. She received top honors at the county level, never dreaming she would go on to become state champion. Everyone was proud of her accomplishment.

"That's one good thing about 4-H," Diane said. "There's something for everyone."

"I'm sure it was planned from the beginning," Diane went on, "that God would give us this beautiful girl who is so gentle and full of love, yet still able to administer discipline and love at the same time to children—any child."

Lisa also loves reading and has a flair for poetry. Her great-grandmother Delzell, Lyn Fehlman's mother, had poetry published and was also a talented artist. In 1980 when she was fourteen, Lisa wrote the following poem about her feelings for her family:

A Family

A family is peace, a place to cry and laugh and vent frustrations,
    to ask for help and tease,
    to be touched and hugged, and smiled at.

A family is people who care when you are sad,
    who love you no matter what,
    who are sharing your triumphs,
    who don't expect you to be perfect,
    just growing with honesty in your own direction.

A family is a circle where we can learn to like ourselves,
where we can learn to make good decisions,
where we can learn to think before we go,
where we can learn integrity,
table manners, respect for other people, for all are special,
where we share ideas, where we listen and are listened to,
where we learn the rules of life to prepare ourselves for the
      world.
The world is a place where anything can happen.
If we grow up in a loving family, we are ready for the world.

A home is a refuge upon which to lay your weary body to
      rest, your concerns of the world,
to get out of the cold, hostile world.
A family is trust, where there's always a shoulder to cry on,
where there's always time for you as an individual.

A family is love every time of the day.

Donny, the "miracle child" described earlier, was next in birth order among the biological children.

The shigella virus Diane caught from Mandy when she was two months pregnant with Diana concerned her, but the baby arrived on October 29, 1978, and she seemed to be a healthy little girl—the Nasons' second home-grown daughter. Diana was a beautiful, dark-haired baby with big, brown eyes and long, black eyelashes. Grandma Fehlman kept remarking how much she looked like Diane when she was little.

The following excerpt from an article Diane wrote for the adoption publication *Because We Care* explains some of the beauty of having both biological and adopted children:

> With sixteen children at home and the oldest being eighteen and the youngest eighteen months, with children from all over the world, many with serious handicaps—you can

imagine the comments when it became evident that Number Seventeen was on the way. We just smiled, many times through clenched teeth, and said, 'this baby is planned.'

Little Miss Seventeen arrived October 29 and has become one of this family's greatest blessings. Diana Louise, our youngest bio-child of five, was indeed planned—planned by Mom and Dad since brother Donny arrived two years ago and planned by God as He knew these late bloomers would add a new dimension of love and understanding to the family.

Dennis and I find that in our large family of children of every nationality with handicaps ranging from mental retardation to muscular dystrophy, it is so important that we see all levels of development and participation. It helps keep our perspective and emotions on an even keel. It gives us patience and motivation to continue in adoptions as a constant uplift.

My two "normal" kids helped me through the trying times. God knew I needed them to balance our family. I decided to write this after reading an article on biological kids. I have written about my adopted twelve, but perhaps it's time to mention those terrific bio-kids, too.

When our oldest son brought all the children up to the hospital to view little Diana there were many comments. The best came from Kecia, our five-year-old Vietnamese daughter.

She had ordered my doctor to have me eat lots of brownies so the baby would be brown like her. She took a long look through the nursery window and finally said, "Well, at least she has black hair." Yes, the Lord took care of that small detail, and on a tiny, fair-skinned babe He put a shock of black hair that you wouldn't believe. The nurses on duty had heard of our family, and, after their visit to see the baby, I overheard the nurses saying, "They are all just beautiful."

Yes, they are beautiful, and the "Peewee Princess," as her daddy calls her, is no exception.

But the little girl, small-boned and delicate, soon showed signs characteristic of the severely allergic.

"Dr. Bill, I've tried everything I could think of," Diane cried. "I can't bear to think of another baby like Mark." Yet she knew the Lord was there to turn to. Besides, she'd been through it already and knew exactly what to expect, what to do when Diana woke in the middle of the night with phlegm so thick it choked her.

The rocking chair was put to use again, as Diane got up with the fretful, sickly baby.

From formula to formula, they tried them all from pre-digested to meat base to goat's milk. Nothing worked. Diana was constantly throwing up or having diarrhea. Pediolite, sugar, water, mineral liquid, and pure apple juice were eventually all she could tolerate.

Diane fed her every two hours, trying to see if a little in her tummy would stay down. That only worked for a few weeks. Diane would hold the terribly sick baby many times a day and pray, "Lord, don't let this baby be so sick. I don't know how she can keep living like this."

"I won't put her in the hospital on IVs and in an oxygen tent," Diane said. "We'll find the answer. I'll have her tested at a specialty clinic to see if anything is wrong with her digestive tract."

For one and a half hours, Diana was held down while dye was put through her system and scanned. The results were negative.

Again, God's plan was in action. It was shortly after Diana's birth that Dennis accepted the job as postmaster in Sisters. Though it was a traumatic move, leaving Mom and Dad Fehlman and Dr. Bill, their dear friend and doctor for so many years, the higher mountain altitude was good for Diana.

"When we went back to the valley to visit in Ashland,

she'd get choked up, couldn't keep her food down, and had diarrhea. We'd return to Sisters, and she'd be better," Diane said. "I knew there was more than one reason for our being sent here."

Diana continued to improve in the clear mountain air. There are still nights when she wakens, wheezy and choking for air, but those times are fewer and farther between.

With Diana's terrific eating problems, baby food was out. Diane puréed food bought fresh every day—carrots, applesauce, and chicken—and put the baby on rice cereal. Diana started getting better. Apple juice is her main liquid, and she may never be able to drink milk. Or she might outgrow the allergy, as Mark has.

After Diana's birth and the difficult medical problems they experienced, Diane and Dennis talked about baby Diana being their last 'home-grown' child. They decided to take steps to "make sure." But shortly after they reached that decision, the Lord spoke to Diane and reminded her about the conversation she'd had with Him while riding horseback on the ranch years ago. *There will be four boys and two girls.*

Diane knew there would be one more Nason baby—a boy.

"I didn't know how, or when, or if I would have the energy, but I knew the Lord wanted us to have another child, so He'd provide the needed energy. And I knew, too, that the child would be a tremendous blessing and addition to our family."

In the fall of 1979 the Nasons participated in a television program about adoption called "Room for One More." Cameramen from KOIN-TV in Portland arrived in Ashland to film the show.

Diane did not want the family to be exploited, but the producer's motives seemed good. They wanted to do a documentary on children in large families and the adoption procedure. The Nasons prime concern is that more people know about adoption and about children who wait to be adopted, so this was a way to reach a larger audience.

This program later received the Odyssey Foundation award in New York City for the best short children's documentary on TV that year. It was an honor, and the Nasons were pleased when they heard the news. They were more surprised and thrilled when the call came asking that the family, including Dennis and Diane, travel to New York to attend a banquet in their honor.

"Wow!" exclaimed Diane. "Do you know what they're asking? You don't automatically pick up a family of eighteen kids and travel clear across the United States. Think of the cost!"

Plans were made. Once again, Diane felt the rigors of being pregnant, but not many people knew about her condition.

Thirteen children went to New York. Diane's brother Jerry came from Idaho to stay at the farm and help with milking and feeding the animals, plus supervising the five remaining kids.

Besides attending the banquet, the Nasons were to appear on a national TV program. The banquet was covered by media from forty different states—TV cameras, reporters, and writers.

It wasn't until that evening just before the program started that the person in charge came rushing up and said, "Oh, by the way, Mrs. Nason, you're the keynote speaker."

Diane's mouth fell open. But only for a minute. The fact that she hadn't been warned, which would have unnerved most people, only fazed her briefly.

"When it comes to talking on adoption and the needs of children overseas and right here in America, I could talk forever," she admits.

She knew that the people in the audience could do some good. Diane realized, too, that this was why the Lord had put them there. He had taken the Nasons through all the upheavals, the waiting, the red tape, the whole bit—to help others.

Diane talked for forty minutes.

"I talked about our lifestyle, about adoption and the children who wait needlessly. I also talked about legislation that can actually block the adoption process; about agencies that promote foster care rather than adoption."

And the audience listened.

One reporter from Georgia came up to Diane later. "Mrs. Nason, I'm going to print what you said, tell how it is. I'm going to start an investigation about why these children aren't being released, why we can't get funding to support more groups, parent groups who advocate adoption. I'm going to hold meetings and try to get people to become aware of the need."

Diane felt rewarded. She'd made people aware of the problem. Now something might be done. If only one person responded as the reporter had, it was worth it.

The Nasons went home, but their trials and problems continued. Diane, stricken with pneumonia, spent a week in the hospital, refusing medication because of her pregnancy. Soon a Down's syndrome baby they had just adopted became ill, was hospitalized, and died a few weeks later. And then came her father's accident and untimely death. Suddenly Diane realized she hadn't felt the baby move for several days.

Following an examination, the doctor tried to monitor the baby's heartbeat. Nothing. He tried for ten minutes until the batteries wore down. Still nothing.

"I don't know what to tell you," he said with a shake of his head. "I know you've been through a lot of stress and strain, and I hate to lay this on you too, but I can't find the heartbeat. You say you haven't felt the baby move all week long?"

"No," Diane said, her mouth trembling. "I haven't."

"There's a possibility that the baby has died and the actual miscarriage hasn't occurred."

Diane controlled her emotions, but once home, she collapsed. She called Dennis at work. "You've got to come home. I can't accept this. Too much has happened these past few months . . ."

But no, she *wouldn't* accept it. Being the fighter that she is, she lay on her bed, praying for a sign. *Lord, this baby is important to us. During these times of trial and death and uncertainty, he's been our ray of hope. He's our tiny miracle of life and we need him. We really need him right now.*

That night Diane felt the baby move. Not once, which could have been a false alarm, but two, then three times. She woke Dennis. "He moved. I felt him."

Dennis bolted up. "Oh, honey, I hope so. Let's go back to the doctor tomorrow."

But when Diane called, the doctor said he'd see her in a week.

"I can't wait a week," she said. "I've got to know *now*."

She went right in.

The doctor attached the monitor and heard a heartbeat loud and clear. Tears of happiness ran down Diane's cheeks. "What do you think happened?"

The doctor looked puzzled. "I can't say for sure. It's very rare, but I've heard of babies going into shock. He must have gone low and deep into the uterus making it impossible to detect a heartbeat. He didn't move because he was almost in shock due to the reactions your body's gone through lately. I've never seen it before, but frankly, it's the only explanation I can think of."

"Will it affect the baby?"

"No, it shouldn't." He patted Diane's shoulder. "I know you're going through a lot, but try to take it a little easier, okay?"

The doctor's findings had given Diane the faith and uplift she needed. With God's strength she knew she would make it through the remainder of the pregnancy. It was her last baby to carry, but he was important in view of the recent losses the family had suffered. This baby would mean so much to so many people.

The last biological Nason, Kenneth Christian, was born on June 27, 1980. The *Kenneth* was for a friend in adoptions, Ken Lucas, Norma's husband, and *Christian* came from the Fehlman side of the family, where the name goes back five generations—or is it two thousand years?

It was a special day, all the more special because Kenny shared the birthdate with Katie, who was ten years old.

Kenny was the picture of health, a replica of Scott, just as Donny had been almost identical to Mark. Kenny had no asthma problems such as Diana had. The Lord knew Diane needed a healthy baby about then. Hadn't there been enough heartbreak?

The last "home-grown" child. The Lord had fulfilled His promise and there they were—the first three "home-grown," the second three "home-grown." All the gaps between had been filled with children He had chosen from all over the world.

Diane's biggest disappointment was that her father was not alive to see this latest addition. She regrets that Kenny will never experience the closeness to his grandpa that Donny had or be held like Diana and the older ones.

Donny felt the same concern. One day while riding in the car he climbed into the back seat next to his younger brother and said, "Don't worry, Kenny. I'll tell you all about your grandpa. Then you'll know him just like I did."

Chapter Fourteen

Danny's Prayer

For a year and a half, Diane had been trying to pry loose from El Salvador a boy named Louis. Danny had prayed for a brother from his country—maybe Louis was the one!

Diane wrote and requested documents and even asked someone going to that country on business to look into the paperwork. Documents were lost—there was no birth certificate—and when a birth certificate was made up, Louis's age was listed as fourteen, too old to be adopted according to his country's rules.

Still Danny prayed.

One day Diane received a call from Lya, her adoption colleague from Georgia. "Diane, I know of a replaced child [one who has already been adopted then rejected] who is available. He's from El Salvador and was adopted there by a couple in the army. He's five now, and they can't keep him. They say he has temper tantrums, steals, and lies. He was abused in El Salvador. He had burns on his body and was a street boy. His name is Carlos."

"Oh, Lya," Diane exclaimed. "This must be the brother Danny's been praying for. What's the procedure with him?"

"The family is searching for a new home for him, but they won't give him up to just anybody. They want a Christian family, and that's when I thought of you."

"I know he's a Nason, Lya," Diane said. "I'll see about getting an update on our home study and get back to you."

The agency staff hit the ceiling. They refused to offer their support. They felt the Nasons should still try to get Louis out, no matter how bleak it looked. They were certain they could place Carlos with a hundred other people because he was still fairly young.

For thirty days, Dennis and Diane could do nothing. Although they felt Carlos was Danny's brother, it appeared Carlos would probably be placed with someone else. At the end of the thirty days, it was confirmed that the Nasons could not proceed in El Salvador. There was no point in trying any further.

One night they received a phone call from Nebraska. The people on the other end said, "Hello, this is Dick and Linda. We are Carlos's parents."

Diane was stunned. She had never expected to hear from the parents. Lya had filled them in on the information about why the Nasons couldn't go ahead and about the size of the Nason family.

"We're Christians, and we believe that you are to be our Carlos's parents. We want you to have him."

"We want him too," Diane said, "and we fully believe that he is our little boy. But there is no way we can work with this agency."

"We know," they said. "We heard and understand the reason, and that's why we withdrew our release for Carlos. We want you to adopt him independently and privately."

"Praise the Lord!" Diane cried. She had known he was their child all along but didn't know how in the world the Lord was going to work it out. This was the answer. He had impressed upon those people that the Nasons were the family for Carlos, so they had decided to take matters into their own hands.

In private adoption, a couple must go through an attorney. The state finalizes the adoption by signing a release. As long as the parents have signed with an attorney as witness, there isn't any problem.

Dick and Linda said they would drive from Nebraska. They had a biological girl and an adopted Caucasian boy. They wanted to meet the Nasons.

Carlos was nearly identical to Danny. They were the same age and size, and were in the same grade of school. They fit together, and along with Kecia, they would be starting the second grade.

Carlos's name was changed to Daryl John—the John after Dennis's grandfather.

The Lord had moved Daryl without the help of an agency. He'd removed all obstacles and answered a little boy's prayers. Neither Dennis nor Diane had anything to do with it.

Diane knew about Daryl's problems and why the family felt they couldn't keep him; but as she pored over the medical records, she couldn't find reasons for the problems. After reading several hundred forms through the years, including medical and psychological evaluations on children, Diane has learned to search for the truth and ignore the labels. Sometimes the problem is with an adult rather than the child.

After arriving at the Nasons' in May 1979, Daryl didn't appear to have any serious difficulties. He was a live wire, no doubt about that. He could get huffy too. When he was spanked, he wouldn't cry. He had a lot of love to give. Most of the time he was one big smile with greenish brown eyes and a mop of hair. His grin would melt your heart.

Dennis and Diane dealt with Daryl the same as they did their other children, though his was a different adoption. Because he was a replacement child he developed a "water off the duck's back" attitude. It was as if he felt, "It won't hurt me. Do whatever you want to."

But inside was a soft-hearted little boy. Dennis and Diane gave him a lot of love and watched his behavior. He took a few cookies and tried to get away with some other things, but he appeared to be testing his new parents and to want attention most of all. The Nasons were consistent in what they believed and in their rules.

All of the children have chores. Daryl was given the job of helping Danny water the cows and bring in the wood. He had to be reminded of certain things, such as, "Yes, you do have to pick up your clothes and hang them up, and yes, you do change your underwear every day."

Daryl still seeks attention. It's just one way to reassure himself that the Nasons really do want him, no matter what he does. He is a bright boy and feels good about himself. His schoolwork is improving, too. He is a blessing and a contributing member of the family.

"Yes," Dennis and Diane agree. "It is amazing to see the different ways the Lord has of 'bringing children home,' and the case of Daryl John Nason is a perfect example."

Chapter Fifteen

The Down's Syndrome Blessings

In 1976, Diane helped place several Down's syndrome children into adoptive homes. Down's syndrome is a genetic disorder resulting in a degree of retardation and some physical abnormalities. At one time these children were considered unadoptable, and many vegetated in institutions and foster care homes. But, it has been discovered in recent years that early stimulation and programming, coupled with love, achieve wonders with Down's babies.

"Don, are you sure you and Sheryl can handle another special needs child?" Diane asked one summer afternoon.

The Nasons had helped this young couple a year earlier in their adoption of little Mark, a Down's baby with many medical problems. Now they were interested in Cindy, a three-year-old girl with the same disorder.

"We love Marky so much," Don answered. "I'm sure we can include Cindy in our family."

Six months later, Don lost his job, and the couple found they didn't have enough time or energy to adopt. They came to Dennis and Diane heartbroken because they felt they must let Cindy return to foster care. In conference with the placement agency, it was decided that the Nasons would keep Cindy until another home could be found.

Cindy lived with the Nasons for two months during 1977, and their experience with her became a steppingstone in their stairway of learning. She was then adopted by a lovely Oregon family who just wanted a little girl to love.

Four years earlier, Diane had met Janet Marchese from New York, through the adoption hot line, a listing of people advocating the adoption of hard-to-place children. Janet had adopted a beautiful Down's baby boy and since that time had directed many families toward the adoption of Down's children. Being coworkers in this area of special needs, Diane and Janet were excited about the amazing results in these childrens' lives.

Early in December 1979, Janet called Diane. "I've got this beautiful baby boy, Diane. He's just three weeks old, and the parents absolutely cannot accept the fact he has Down's syndrome. Would you and Dennis be interested in him? They just want a private adoption."

"We've been praying about the Down's children for so long, and we both agree we want to include these children in our family," Diane answered. "Yes, he's ours," she said later, after conferring with Dennis.

Since the Nasons had just returned from the awards banquet for the Odyssey Foundation in New York, Lahna Rasmussen, a friend in adoptions, offered to fly back and pick up little Martin Paul, the name the Nasons picked out for the baby.

When Diane first looked at their beautiful new son in the yellow bunny suit, he smiled. He had bright little eyes, a turned-up nose, and a bit of light brown hair. *Oh, how could they give him up?* she wondered. *He's just a beautiful gift from God.*

For five days the family had a wonderful time with little Marty. Since all the bedrooms were full at the time, Marty's cradle was placed in the large, upstairs guest bathroom, giving him sleeping privacy.

One night Lisa asked, "Mom, can he sleep downstairs in my room tonight? I'll give him his bottle."

"Sure, honey," Diane said, "if it means a lot to you."

Dennis's sister Sherri and her husband, Terry, visited during those five days. They had been married several years, but were dubious about having children. Shortly after arriving, they walked into the guest bathroom and found Marty asleep in the cradle. He awakened suddenly and smiled.

"Dennis is ready to go," Diane called up the stairs. "What's taking you two so long?"

Sherri came down the stairs with Marty in her arms.

"Oh, was he awake?" Diane asked.

"Yes," Sherri answered. "He's so beautiful, and he looks at you with such trust."

"I know. Aren't we lucky? He's a special baby, and I really believe he was sent by God," Diane responded. "He's already touched many hearts."

Sherri and Terry returned home, and the Nasons later learned the young couple had discussed having children the whole four-hour trip home and decided they wanted a baby.

On the fifth day of Marty's life with the Nasons, he developed diarrhea. When it continued more than a day, Diane took him to see a pediatrician.

"He's getting a bit raw from the diarrhea," the doctor said.

"I know," Diane said. "He doesn't weigh that much, and I'm really worried about him."

"Maybe it's the flu. He could have picked up something on the plane. I'll take some tests."

But Marty didn't improve. Diane called the doctor again the next day. "He's quit eating now. I'm worried about his losing more weight and becoming dehydrated. I want him put in the hospital."

The doctor agreed and asked her to bring him over that afternoon.

A day later Marty was desperately ill and the doctor discovered that a blood vessel had burst in his brain. He was on IVs and tubes were poked in him. Additional tests were taken. There was a weakness, a malformation which couldn't have been detected and could have happened any time. Marty's brain cavity was filling with blood and doing extensive damage to his brain tissue.

The Nasons prayed; people in the church prayed; Norma Lucas and other friends in adoption prayed. Janet was on the phone every day. Marty had affected her family so much the night he was there. Her little boy had never stopped talking about Marty, although her family had known many Down's children.

Marty's condition worsened. The doctors said they didn't know why he was still alive. Dennis and Diane held him just to let him know he had love and warmth. They talked to him, hoping some of their love would strengthen him. He rallied off and on and seemed to respond to their touch, but the brain damage was massive and no operation could be performed. He continually lost weight. The doctors spoke with the Nasons about unhooking the IVs and giving him liquids by mouth so he wouldn't dehydrate. One doctor felt that Marty would die the next day. But he didn't; he was a fighter.

During Marty's hospitalization, Diane received a call from Ashland. It was her dad.

"Diane, I want you to know I'm praying for you and little Marty."

Here was another person Marty had touched in his short

life. Grandpa Fehlman believed in the Lord, but being a private person, he didn't usually mention his practice of prayer.

After he hung up, Diane remembered a poem her dad had written. *We're so much alike,* she thought, *putting our thoughts down on paper.*

Tired and Sleepy

I'm tired and sleepy, I'm so tired and sleepy.
So tuck me in my little bed and leave me there alone to rest.
Up high in the sky among the bright stars. Up high with my
    God, I'll sleep in His arms.
So tuck me to sleep, to dreamland I'll go.
To that faraway land where babies are safe in God's arms.
He loaned me to you from His Heaven above.
To show you the goodness that comes from above.
The love that I get came from Him up above.
Up high in the sky where the infinite reigns.
He sent me to you . . . a symbol of love.
To have and to hold and be nearer your God.
So tuck me to sleep in my own little bed.
The stars that shine down from Him up above will guide us
    all there when He calls us back home.

It was signed "Grandpa," and dated December 1, 1962, with the inscription: "To all my grandchildren."

Little did he know then that this poem would have an impact on his life when he was seventy-four years old.

The technicians and nurses continued to marvel at how Marty hung on. But God knew Marty would touch a few more hearts in this world.

One was the heart of the therapist who administered Marty's brainwave tests in the hospital.

Dennis went with Marty for many of the tests. During

one of the tests, he was talking about how the Lord had touched a lot of people through little Marty. The technician listened. He knew about the Nasons and how Marty had arrived into their home, as the doctor had shared the story with many people.

"I don't see how this baby is still alive," the technician said.

"Miracles do happen," Dennis said. "Plus, maybe Marty's work here on earth isn't done yet."

"You really believe that God would allow this to happen?" the man asked.

"Hey," Dennis broke in, "God doesn't allow this to happen. This is the world. There's sickness and illness and that's the world. We're all going back someday, and the Christians will go back and be with the Lord. If that's what He wants for Marty, then that's the way it will be—though it's earlier than we'd wish."

"That's the kind of faith I want to have," the man said. "This little baby has really touched me, too, ever since he came into the hospital. I'm going to try harder to live my life by faith."

On January 8, Dennis and Diane took all the children to the hospital. They knew Marty's condition was grave and had prayed continuously for the infant. The older children had visited before, and now the hospital granted permission for all the children to come.

Marty was down to four pounds. His little head had been shaved for all the tests, but he wasn't on any artificial life support. He was still beautiful.

The children knew this was their baby brother. They also knew he was very ill. He didn't respond to anything. They needed to know he would soon be in a better place. They didn't want him to be that ill here on earth when he could be a whole, smiling, happy baby with Jesus.

They all held him. It was especially hard on Lisa as she was old enough to know Marty was gravely ill. But she needed to see Marty this one last time.

Kecia touched his hand and gave him a kiss.

Marty died three days later on January 11, 1980. He was with Jesus, and it was time to rejoice. A memorial service was given at church.

It was another time of letting go in the Nasons' lives. But it is always harder with a little baby.

As the Nasons reflected on what Marty had done in the short time he was their son, they knew why God had sent him. He had touched numerous people. He was a beautiful advocate of Down's syndrome children—their needs, abilities, and potential.

Marty had helped a young couple to decide on taking a chance and having a baby. He had showed a grandpa more love. He had touched the hearts of people in Oregon, stewardesses on the airplane bringing him to Oregon, and families in New York.

Diane received calls from people who had heard in Down's syndrome foundations across the country. A lady in Minnesota who had lost a Down's baby to a heart defect phoned the Nasons.

The Nasons will always be grateful that Marty came into their lives and that they were the ones who were privileged to share his life on earth for whatever length of time. He was six weeks old when he died. He had spent three weeks in the hospital, five days in their home, and would remain forever in their hearts.

On February 25, 1981, exactly one year after Grandpa Fehlman died, a new life began in the Nason family. On that date they picked up little Kevin Martin Nason at the airport and welcomed him into their family.

The five days preceding Kevin's arrival had been a busy

time for the Nasons. They had made the six-hour round trip to Portland, where three hours had been spent in Immigration and Naturalization Service procedures. Danny, Daryl, and Mandy officially became United States citizens.

After driving home in a snowstorm, the Nasons received a call from Janet in New York.

"You're not going to believe what I have, Diane," she said. "I have heard about a baby boy in Florida—a Down's baby—and I understand he's beautiful. The parents cannot accept his handicap and won't even bring him home from the hospital. They want him placed privately with someone."

"They don't want him going into an institution or foster care," Janet went on. "I have a list of people who want Down's babies, but I felt little Marty was directing me and saying, 'This one's a Nason.' All I could do was dial your number."

Dennis and Diane were absolutely thrilled. It was as if Marty were saying, "Well, I paved the way. Now I am sending another little ambassador down there to tell the world, 'Hey, I can accomplish lots and, hey, I'm somebody, and I'm me.'"

Diane said "yes" right on the phone.

"The parents will pay all the expenses for you to fly back to get him," Janet concluded.

Dennis made arrangements for time off from work for the trip. Diane drove him over to the travel agency in Bend to pick up the ticket.

"Mr. Nason, there's a call for you," the clerk said.

Something must be wrong, Diane thought. The caller was the baby's father. It was a first for them—the first time they'd had contact with a biological parent.

The man wanted to explain that all the hotels around the airport were full, so he was making other arrangements for

Dennis to stay overnight. He seemed nervous, as if he needed reassurance, and Dennis told him they'd talk when he got there.

Diane drove Dennis to Redmond to catch his flight. It was 10:30 A.M. and he was ready to begin the first leg of his journey.

Donny was upset because his daddy was leaving. He still was insecure because of his grandpa's leaving and never coming back.

"Donny, just think," Diane said, putting an arm around her sobbing son. "When daddy comes home, he'll have a beautiful baby brother for you."

"I can't wait to see my baby brother, but is Daddy going to fly real high?" Donny asked.

"Yes, the airplane goes pretty high."

"If he flies by heaven, will he stop and say hello to Grandpa for me?"

Diane felt a lump come to her throat as she nodded. Here was one little boy who still missed his grandpa.

After meeting the biological father, Dennis was able to reassure him that if he couldn't accept his son's handicap, then he was doing the child a favor in giving him up. "Down's children are so loving and require total acceptance and love to blossom and grow," Dennis told him.

Dennis left the hospital early the next morning. After meeting the attorney who processed the adoption papers and receiving a call from Janet in New York, who assured the hospital that Dennis was indeed the baby's adoptive father, Dennis finally held his new son.

Kevin was two weeks old, with beautiful coloring, hair that stuck straight up, and a cute little nose. Dennis proudly wrapped him in the bunting Diane had sent.

Another overnight stay, a call to Diane, and then home at 8:15 Wednesday morning.

Yes, Marty, your namesake, Kevin Martin, is beautiful. He is a blessing to all he meets. He is happy, "right-on" in his development, and a challenge to his preschool teachers. Thank you, Marty, for paving the way, Dennis and Diane agree.

Kevin welcomed his little sister, Cynthia Janet, in November, 1981. They are the same age, look like twins, and share two names: Down's syndrome and Nason.

Chapter Sixteen

How Does a
Large Family Work?

How do the Nasons manage a home for such a passel of kids? While many women are breathing heavy sighs of relief because the last child is finally off to school and they can wash the jelly off the walls for good, Diane is busy signing papers to bring yet another child into her home. How can she find so much time, love, and energy?

Work that would tire most people out is nothing to Diane. She has an inner strength, an extra amount of love, eyes in the back of her head—as her children can tell you— and a super sensitive pair of ears. She knows what each child is doing and where each child is—whether inside or outside. One tiny whimper and she knows which baby it is and who is responsible for the baby on that day. Usually saying the name once in a stacatto way is all that is necessary to remind the older child of his responsibility.

Diane loves being active. She *is* active. She makes things run smoothly. It would be next to impossible for anyone to step in and take over where Diane left off. She has a terrific memory. She can spout off her children's names, birthdates, and the year each one "came home."

The Nason home is clean, not antiseptic like a hospital, but uncluttered. Everything has a place, and that is where it goes.

A collection of frogs lines the shelves under the big picture windows in the living room. They belong to Diane.

On the windowsill above the kitchen sink are mugs handmade by some of the children over the years. Each has a cactus in it. In the middle, in Diane's view where she spends so much of her time, is a small dough picture frame. "Number one Grandparents," it says. In it is the Nasons' first grandchild—Mark and Terri's little girl, Nicole, the start of a new generation of Nasons.

The bulletin board and walls in the kitchen and hall are covered with posters. One depicts a frog and says: *I like you just the way you are.*

One of Diane's favorites shows a child in a highchair and says: *God loves you and I'm trying.*

The poster that sums up Diane and Dennis's philosophy for what they are doing shows a baby with his foot in his mouth and says: *The whole theory of the universe comes down to one life, one day at a time.*

The Nason dining room is typical of the old-time parlors where people entertained. The room is filled with antiques Diane has collected. Heavy oak cabinets are filled with green Depression glass. Old blue enamelware sits on the antique kerosene cookstove. An oxen yoke graces another wall, and family pictures are exhibited in large wooden frames. Branding irons from the ranch hang on a wall, and a stack of children's activities magazines adds to the mementos.

The room is off-limits to the children. "Children by permission only," Diane says. "Children need to understand that some things are for adults only."

"Do some of the children get lost in the shuffle?" is a question frequently asked.

Absolutely not. To Diane, each child is a unique individual with a distinct personality. Each has his or her own bed and a special place for belongings. Besides clothing, these include a baby book and scrapbook filled with memorabilia concerning the child's beginnings—a picture at birth, if possible, news clippings—anything that describes that child's heritage.

Another possession that is proudly displayed in the child's bedroom is a personal collection.

Daryl collects baseball cards and he has over five hundred.

Lisa has antique dolls of all sizes from all over the world.

Theresa likes Smurfs.

Lori has a large collection of horses.

Jeff collects stamps.

Melissa and Mandy both like dolls and bears.

Kecia likes anything that is "Strawberry Shortcake."

There is a "sharing-game" closet, but certain things belong to each child and don't have to be shared.

"Their various interests and collections give us suggestions for gifts at birthdays and Christmas," Diane explained. "We always have a big celebration on each child's birthday."

Diane loves to decorate cakes. She's made train cakes for the boys, carousel cakes, Raggedy Ann and Andy cakes, and many other unique designs. She strives for ideas that make each child feel special. The kids make elaborate birthday cards to give. Sometimes they stick in a few pennies or give up a special belonging, such as a pretty rock or picture.

People continue to shake their heads in astonishment and ask the inevitable questions. How can the Nasons do it? How can they afford it? How does Diane find the time? She must have help. She's got to have outside help.

Diane does not have household help. The older children babysit or fill in at times of need, such as the times when

Diane has been ill—with shigella, following the birth of a baby, or with pneumonia.

What about the mornings when the older children are at school, when the only ones home are the preschoolers and the babies in diapers? Who helps out then?

"It takes organization," Diane says. "Everything is done systematically."

When it's time for a diaper change, Diane starts with the youngest, Kevin, then goes to Billy, Cindy, and Kenny.

"It only takes about five minutes unless one of them has dirty pants."

The same goes for their feeding time. She feeds all four babies at once, then they all go down for a nap.

The preschoolers are kept busy with morning activities once "Sesame Street" goes off the TV.

One morning they play with their toys. There is interchanging and sharing. Another morning it might be Legos or blocks. A third morning it's coloring books, puzzles, and picture books. There are always Christian tapes or nursery rhymes playing.

"You need planned activity with several children," Diane explains. "Not everything is structured, however. On nice days, they might go out to play on the swing set. When the older ones are at home, they may start a game of baseball."

There are horses for the older children to ride, and cats and dogs for the little ones to enjoy. No animals come inside, due to Diana's allergies.

The Nasons have twenty acres, about five miles east of the town of Sisters. That acreage holds about twenty-five cows, two dogs (both Saint Bernards), six cats, thirty chickens, two horses, twelve calves, and twenty-one rabbits.

A three-bedroom house came with the property, and shortly afterward the Nasons added four bedrooms, plus a family room with cribs lined along two of the walls.

"Within a large family there are rules that must be followed," Diane says. "No home can run without rules and regulations. Even a small child learns at an early age what he can touch and what he can't. He learns that he cannot bite, hit, or be selfish with his toys."

The Nasons have rules for everything and believe in strict enforcement.

"Consistency is important in a child's life, no matter who he is, or what the age," Dennis states.

Each child has a job or task to perform. The four older girls each take charge of a baby in the mornings. They change, feed, and dress the infant for the day. Sometimes they also change the crib sheet.

Children are assigned to set and clear the table. Others wash and put the dishes away. The jobs are rotated so nobody gets bored. Clothes are folded and put into the proper bins. Beds are made each morning.

"I feel strongly about the children eating a hot breakfast before leaving for school," Diane says. There are several menus to interchange: scrambled eggs with sausage or bacon, toast, juice, and milk; a big pot of oatmeal; pancakes or french toast. On weekends the children eat cold cereal, and Diane gets a break.

"We get through four gallons of milk a day and up to four loaves of bread, depending on what we have for breakfast," Diane said.

Typical Nason Dinner Menus

Beef stew	Pork chops
Biscuits or bread	Cornbread
Pudding or fruit	Green beans
Roast chicken	Turkey and dressing
Biscuits, gravy	Potatoes
Canned vegetable	Vegetable

Pot roast	Chili dogs
Potatoes, carrots	Fruit salad
Gravy	
	Rice
Spaghetti	Meat or vegetable casserole
French bread	
Tossed green salad	

A casserole for dinner at the Nasons requires three 8″ x 13″ pans.

Diane does the shopping after the older kids are home. She and the girls bake pastries and freeze a week's supply.

Fruits and vegetables are purchased in gallon containers from the local grocery store. The owner places special orders as the Nasons need them. Big jars of mayonnaise and peanut butter are also bought there. Sometimes Diane gets a good buy on certain cuts of beef from the local butcher.

Food is one of the family's biggest expenses, plus the loan on the house and acreage. The Nasons could qualify for food stamps and free lunches at school, but they decline to accept such aid. Why?

"We want our children to grow up being self-sufficient, not looking to the government for a handout," Dennis says. "We believe in the principle of working for what we get. We adopted these kids because we wanted them, so we'll take care of them too."

One thing that impresses a visitor to the Nason house is the quietness, especially at the table. At Sunday dinner you have to look twice to make sure there are twenty-four people seated around the table. It's peaceful. There are no slurps, sniffs, or talking with a full mouth, no complaints of, "He got the biggest roll!" Nobody hassles anyone.

Fighting among siblings is held at a minimum all the time. An occasional glare might be seen from one child to another, and a poke now and then, but there are none of the gripes or whines often heard among children like: "He hit me!" or, "Make him stop looking at me."

The secret behind this peaceful mealtime is enforcement. Any infraction at the table or elsewhere gets the offender restricted to his or her room, and, as everyone knows, children like to eat.

But more importantly, there is love, a gentle coaxing to get little ones to eat, and always Diane's hearty laugh can be heard.

Diane no longer gardens or cans food. "It isn't feasible here in Sisters," Dennis said. "The growing season is so short—just the three summer months. Even then, there has been frost as late as June and as early as August."

"Besides, nobody has come up with an eight-quart jar, which is what I need for fruit," Diane quips. "It's easier, quicker, and cheaper to buy by the gallon at the bulk food store."

Before they moved from Ashland, Diane canned more than six hundred quarts of fruit and vegetables every year. The Nasons also raised their own pork, beef, chickens, and rabbits, plus Scott's cow for milk. But that was when they were a family of twelve.

How do they clothe twenty-four kids?

"We buy shoes," Diane says, "but most of the clothing is donated, except items of clothing for birthdays or special occasions. It's wonderful the way people have always sent things. Many are hand-me-downs, but in good condition."

A dress manufacturer in Florida saw an article about the Nasons and wrote to them, asking for the sizes of all the girls.

"A month later a huge box arrived with three dresses for each girl. They were just beautiful, and in time for Easter."

Diane leafed through an album and brought out a picture of the girls in their new dresses. "We sent a picture to the owner and a letter of thanks."

"We have always taught the children to give rather than to receive," Diane added, "but we think it is important to be able to receive graciously, too."

One of the biggest chores is the massive laundry created by a family the size of the Nasons.

When the Nasons lived in Ashland, the washers and dryers had a service contract. If anything went wrong, the company came out and fixed it. But the small town of Sisters doesn't have a company that offers a contract. Now when the washer breaks down, unless it's a minor problem, the Nasons must purchase a new machine. (The machines usually last about a year—until the week after the warranty runs out.)

The children are conservative with their clothes. Jeans aren't dirty after one wearing, but underwear and socks are changed daily. If dresses are hung up, and shirts and pants folded properly, they can be worn again.

The babies wear disposable diapers. They are a major expense, but they help reduce the laundry and give Diane more time for other jobs.

Each child bathes twice a week, and washes his or her hair on one of those nights. Again, the older ones assist the younger children by running the water, checking for dirty ears, and shampooing hair.

Everyone helps someone else. Except for the tiniest babies, each child can find another one to help in some way. That's what the Nasons want to impress on their children: A family works together, plays together, rejoices and grieves together. Their motto is: *You are never alone.*

What parent doesn't relish the time of day when the children are safely tucked into bed for the night? Dennis and Diane are no different. Those precious few evening hours are the only time they have together—uninterrupted. Diane has a definite bedtime hour for all. It may seem early, but people in this area also get up early.

7:00 P.M. for the little ones in diapers.
7:30 P.M. for kindergarten through third grade.
8:00 P.M. older grade-schoolers
9:00 P.M. junior high and high schoolers.

Some of the older kids may read or do homework in their rooms until a later hour.

Since Dennis is a gourmet who loves cooking, he and Diane cook together on special days such as Thanksgiving and Christmas dinners. She cooks the rest of the time, assisted by the older girls. Lisa can whip up a meal for twenty-six in nothing flat.

In 1978, the Nasons took a trip to Gold Beach on the Oregon coast. They swapped houses with friends who lived there, making it an inexpensive vacation.

During the summer of 1981, the whole family traveled in their van to Eureka, California to visit Dennis's father and his side of the family.

"It was the first time we'd been there in five years," Diane recalled.

They put sleeping bags on the floor and converted the garage to an eating hall. They might have stayed longer than two days, but the weather was horrible and the kids couldn't even go to the beach.

"It was still a good visit and the kids got to see cousins, aunts, uncles, and grandparents," Dennis said.

"We also go on fishing trips, or picnics and swimming for the day," Diane added. "They are family excursions. We pile into the van and head for one of the rivers."

The family attends the state fair each year, as several of their kids have exhibits on display. Now that Mark lives in Portland, they travel there to see him twice a year. The rest of the time everyone is too busy to think about vacation.

Besides the usual school activities, the kids are busy with church youth groups and 4-H work.

"We have our own 4-H group right here at home," Diane said. "I teach the girls cooking and handicrafts. Each girl can plan and cook a meal. Some of them raise calves."

The older kids go skating in Bend in the winter and swimming in the summer.

Diane doesn't believe in allowances. "Children shouldn't be paid to do jobs. It's a responsibility, a learning process, the cogs that make a family work. Each must do his or her part to make the family run smoothly. Kids shouldn't do chores to receive money—not that money is never given. If a need arises, the child receives funds. It depends on how much money is in the family coffer at the time."

The Nasons do not have a savings account. Any spare money that might accumulate usually goes for repairs on a washing machine, a new hot water tank, or parts for the van.

"We can still all fit into one van," Diane says with a laugh, "but the day is coming when we'll need a bus."

The spirit of competition and striving to excel is also important in the Nason household. The older ones participate in sports, cooking, sewing, and raising calves. "It gives them an incentive to try their hand at whatever interests them most," Diane believes.

"We try to go to as many of their activities as possible," Dennis adds.

Both Dennis and Diane are constantly encouraging their kids to try to do better in school, to do their very best in their jobs.

Some of the older kids have jobs. Lisa works in the Gallery Restaurant, where she is now a backup cook. She leaves for college soon and will major in Christian music and youth ministry.

Theresa works in a supermarket where she is affectionately called "the can girl," since she tends to all the returnable bottles and cans. (Due to Oregon's bottle bill, this particular job is a big one.) Recently, she became a cashier.

In the spring of 1982, Theresa was crowned Central Oregon Dairy Princess.

Diane was jubilant. "Her speech was fantastic! She was poised and confident." Her topic? "The role of aging people in today's society."

Katie, a sixth grader, won many blue ribbons at her school's track meet. This is not a first for Katie, who loves anything athletic. She is also an A-student in an accelerated class for gifted students.

At home Katie is the one who milks all twenty-five cows for Scott when he takes a day off. And she shares an avid interest in photography with her big brother Mark.

Katie's imagination and inventive mind create another challenge to keep up with. "I remember her conversations with a make-believe crowd of five or six at a very early age," Diane said. "They were all different voices. One conversation with Jesus was so typical of Katie.

"Jesus, do you know anyone with purple hair?" Katie asked.

"Yes, I do," (Deep voice from Katie).

"Who?"

"God has purple hair."

"I want to see it."

"I'll lower the rope."

"Whoops! I missed it. Throw it again. Now I got it."

After climbing the rope: "Boy, you really *do* have purple hair. I don't want to stay in heaven. I just want to play here. I'll be back later."

Lisa won a blue ribbon in 1980 at the state fair for her piece-block quilt, which hangs on the wall in Diana's room. Blue and white in color, it features Mother Goose characters. She worked on it for weeks. Her latest project was a dollhouse done in needlepoint, for which she won the grand champion prize at the county fair.

Mark won letters in baseball and football. Before he was well enough to participate in school athletics, he won several trophies in bowling tournaments and ribbons for his photography. At age twenty he manages a store in a large shopping mall near Portland. His goal is to become district manager of many stores in his chain.

Scott went out for wrestling and football, as did Dennis in his high school days. Scott's letters and awards adorn the living room in his mobile home. He also won in music competition with his trombone.

Kari is a good student. Her quiet ways make her especially endearing to others. She often reads the bedtime story to the little ones. In spite of the lack of feeling in her hands as a result of the burns, she practices the flute constantly and plays quite well.

Lori, an outdoor girl, loves horses and enters her calves in 4-H at county fair each year. She has won several blue ribbons for her animals. Some day she hopes to enter in rodeo competition as Diane did. She also enjoys playing the piano and singing.

Kecia, an avid reader, gets good marks in her third grade class and is quite an artist. She is also full of spunk and a class leader in various activities.

Danny loves to read and collects books, and Daryl would like to be a baseball player.

Why are these kids winners?

Is it because Dennis and Diane *care*? Is it because they *expect* a lot and the children try their best to live up to those expectations? Mom and Dad expect them to live and grow to their full potential; each one is different and unique.

Perhaps another reason for the competitive spirit is that

none of the Nasons is afraid to try. There is constant encouragement, not only from Dennis and Diane, but from siblings, too, who exclaim, "You can do it, we *know* you can."

This goes for all, not just kids in school. This cry was heard when Melissa was trying to walk; when Mandy was learning to eat with her feet; when Kevin was beginning to crawl.

There is always someone there, encouraging, coaxing them on to success. When success is reached, the child is openly cheered and praised.

Words from an old western song, "seldom is heard a discouraging word," could be the theme of the Nason clan.

"We also teach them spiritual values," says Dennis. "We take them to church, encourage them to know and accept the Lord. They have all attended Sunday school and church since they were little. We want Christianity to be a way of life for them—for all of us."

Chapter Seventeen

One Day at a Time

The sign extending over the driveway leading to the Nason house says:

PLAINVIEW DAIRY
THE NASONS

If there were room for another sign, it might read:

ONE DAY AT A TIME

That is the philosophy of the Nason family: "Live one day at a time, just as God has given it to us." That motto and the faith it takes to live it go as far back as the time when Mark was a very sick baby and not expected to live past nine years of age.

"Live one day at a time," Dr. Bill Miller told them.

It was the strong, personal Christian faith of Dennis and Diane, never giving up, never letting go, believing that their son *would* get better, that helped Dr. Bill in his walk with the Lord.

"It's up to God now," he'd said that autumn afternoon while Diane paced the floor inside Mark's hospital room.

"Yes, it's up to You, God," Diane repeated.

And through the years, day by day, He has led them. It is this sense of being led that keeps Diane motivated and moving. Once Diane feels a conviction, *she won't give up.*

"I've contacted senators, congressmen, and local civic leaders, because I knew they could become a vital part of the situation, but name-dropping doesn't appeal to me. Why bother when there are so many *real* problems in the world?

"Everything done in life has a purpose," Diane believes. All those hours on the ranch, riding uphill and down, singing praises to God, talking things over with Him, experiencing the abundant life as few have experienced it, helped Diane become the useful vessel she is today. In her younger years, she absorbed a love and appreciation for life, the exhilaration of roaming the ranch and living among God's creatures. She had taken and taken of God's bounty.

From the love of her parents, the careful guidance and moral teaching of her mother, and the communing with God in the open, the molding began. It was as if the Lord had said, "Diane, I need someone who cares, someone who will take care of my children. And, yes, so the burden is not too heavy, there will be someone to help share this load. You will both be young, but together you will learn and grow and reach out in the love I am filling you with."

Yet no matter how much Diane and Dennis try to help the homeless children, how many they take into their home, the task is impossible for them to do alone.

"That is why the message must get out there," Diane insists. "Time is short. Everywhere there are children hurting, starving, wanting love, needing someone who cares about them. Doesn't anyone want to do anything?

"Not everyone can do what we do. Adopting children is not for everyone," Diane acknowledges. "But every Christian can do *something*. There are volunteer jobs. Schools, hospitals, libraries, and nursing homes need help. The list is endless. Wherever there are people, there is a need for help.

"I reflect about the three years since Mandy arrived," Diane continues, "and remember everything that occurred to bring her home. I think about how the Lord moved so many people and used so many in bringing this little girl home. As I reflect on how He has accomplished all He has done in our lives, I remember He brought us children of every nationality.

"Jesus Christ has led us one step at a time, as He has always done with His people. He led us from one adoption to another, from one race to another, from one handicap to another, from one bureaucratic hangup to another, until we knew nearly all the 'ins and outs' of the adoption process.

"The most important thing He did was to unite a family of all nationalities. That was what we had, and we weren't really aware of it. He wanted to show us that the family unit, working together in love and concern for each other, is how He wants His world. I believe that is why the Bible states, 'I will not leave you orphans; I will come to you' (John 14:18).

"I reflect on that and think that I couldn't have done it alone. We believe our family is one of His tools of bringing this about and telling other people about it."

An editor friend who met the Nason family recalled, "When I went to visit the Nason home, I expected it to be a downer. Seeing all those handicapped kids would be depressing. How wrong I was. *I* came away blessed. There was such an atmosphere of love, acceptance, and family unity. It was incredible."

Where is the Lord leading this family? What lies ahead for the children in the little town of Sisters? How many more will join this growing family?

"Only God knows," Dennis says. "And as we continue to listen and seek His guidance, we will see our lives unfold *one day at a time.*"

Epilogue
by Diane Nason

Because our commitment and our dedication to special-needs children continues to grow, the end of this book can only be considered the beginning.

We have a vision, and that vision is of many, many children: children in need, children who don't belong in institutions, children who need the love and security of a Christian family, children who need to start growing in the Lord and knowing Him.

If our work and our vision are to continue and to grow, we have to be open to God's plan. We have been told we are to continue what we are doing—against opposition, against odds that sometimes seem insurmountable. The Lord has said He will hand-pick our children and bring them home to us.

The latest hand-picked Nasons include Billy Joe, who arrived home on January 6, 1982, at the age of one year old. He was deaf, autistic, with a cleft palate, a cleft lip, and hemihypertrophy on the left side. Black and beautiful Billy Joe, now two, is jabbering and running hand in hand with his counterpart—blond, fair, homegrown Kenny.

Nancy, age ten, became a Nason on July 14, 1982. From

Calcutta, India, the victim of severe abuse and emotional deprivation, she's learning what love means and is speaking English with the goal of learning to read. So much healing had to be done, and there's so much yet to go, but God has the upper hand in her life now.

The bright happy smile, softly curled black hair, and black eyes give little clue to Bobby's background of malnutrition, abuse, and cerebral palsy. Bobby, black/white, from New York City, was three and a half years old when he came into our hearts.

And then came Richard, a bright blue-eyed Down's baby from Brazil, who arrived in January 1983. According to the practice sanctioned in Brazil, his biological parents were given the choice at the time of his birth of putting him to death or institutionalizing him because of his Down's syndrome disability. Instead, they chose to fly with him to New York where they heard of our family, called asking us to adopt him, and flew with Richie to Oregon to the waiting arms of his new family.

Only a few short years ago we had envisioned a huge, ranch-style home—somewhat on the order of the hotel-ranch situation where I was reared—where each child can share his or her room with one other person and be a part of the total family unit. With God speaking to and working through one especially dedicated Christian couple and other Christian friends, that vision has become a reality. Our family's home has been expanded to become a seventeen-bedroom home directly facing the three snow-capped peaks—the "sisters" named Faith, Hope, and Charity for which the town of Sisters is named. Now we have the place for our children to explore, to grow, to be close to nature, and to be close to God.

It takes a lot to rebuild the shattered lives of these children. The Lord has given us that chore, that mission, and that vision. He didn't say it would be easy. He didn't say there wouldn't be times when we'd say, "We're just too tired. We just want to rest." And He didn't say there wouldn't be times of great disappointment or times of great sadness.

But He has shown us the path in those times. There are also times of great happiness—exhilarating moments when He performs His miracles, however small or large.

He has promised us and He has shown us that He will take care of these children, that He will provide the food and the clothing and the wherewithal to raise them.

We are the ones who have benefitted from being a part of the family that God built—the Celebration Family.

About the Authors

Besides supervising her large household, Diane Nason remains active in placing homeless children with loving families. She has written numerous articles on adoption and published a cookbook to raise funds for Vietnamese orphans. She and her husband, Dennis, and many children live in Sisters, Oregon.

Birdie L. Etchison is a professional freelance writer. She has written more than four hundred stories and articles, as well as two juvenile books, *Me and Greenley* and the best-selling *Strawberry Mountain*. Currently president of Oregon Christian Writers, she received the 1982 Writer-of-the-Year Award in Juvenile Fiction at Warner Pacific College.